TIMELESS

by

NICHOLAS TCHKOTOUA

Published by

Mta Publications
London

Published by:

Mta Publications
27 Old Gloucester St
LONDON WC1 N3AX
mtapublications@yahoo.co.uk

First published in 1949 by Murray and Gee
Original text © the heirs of Nicholas Tchkotoua
Edited text © Mta Publications and Charles Tchkotoua

All photographs and Introduction © Peter Nasmyth

Cover design Victoria Kirkham

ISBN 9780955914515

CONTENTS

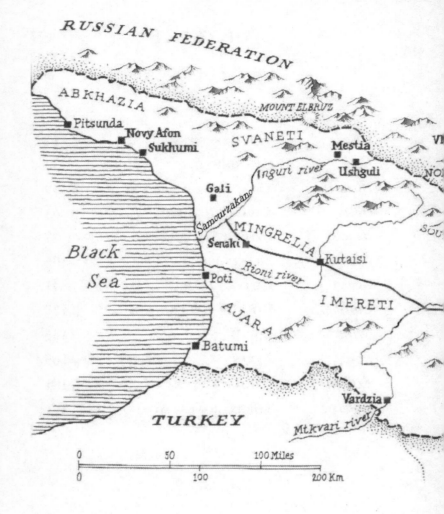

RUSSIAN FEDERATION

ABKHAZIA

MOUNT ELBRUZ

Pitsunda

Novy Afon
Sukhumi

SVANETI

Mestia

Ushgudi

Inguri river

Gali

Samourzakano

MINGRELIA

Senaki

Black
Sea

Rioni river

Kutaisi

Poti

IMERETI

AJARA

Batumi

Vardzia

TURKEY

Mtkvari river

0		50		100 Miles

0   100   200 Km

INTRODUCTION

In May of 1988, a young Georgian woman walked up to the cemetery by the St. Panteleimon church in Tbilisi, the capital city of the then Georgian Soviet Socialist Republic. Accompanying her were two Westerners on their first visit to the Soviet Union. One of them carried a shoulder bag concealing a small casket which they had smuggled past the Moscow customs. Inside that casket lay the heart of a man – now as ashes. They arrived at the elegant 19th century church, with its grand view of the city and Caucasus mountains, knowing they were about to commit an act of defiance against the Soviet authorities. They also knew that their tiny rebellion would amount to probably no more than an unnoticed gesture in the face of the enormous Communist injustice inflicted on this ancient nation for the previous 67 years.

The man whose heart they carried was Nicholas Tchkotoua, the author of this novel. When he left Georgia in 1921 at the age of sixteen, neither he nor his family imagined in their cruellest dreams that their country would become totally sealed off from the world for the next three generations. Nor did he have any inkling that his whole life would turn into one of exile from his cherished home. He, along with so many other Georgian families, had been forced to flee as the Bolshevik army advanced on their country in February 1921. From that day until his death in 1984 he never returned. Indeed until the late 1960s, when limited phone contact was finally allowed, he had made no connection whatsoever with the relatives that stayed behind. Most émigrés feared that any contact with their Sovietised relatives could easily provoke more problems for them than it was worth.

Inevitably, like so many millions of Russian, Georgian, Azeri and Armenian émigrés who had fled the Bolshevik revolution, all his life he nursed a great longing to see again the forbidden land of his childhood. When the slight possibility of a visit opened up in his later years, illness would unfortunately prevent the journey. It was at around this time he requested that his heart at least be buried in the land where it had grown, and where he felt it and he truly belonged.

Although he had planned to write other books, by the time of his death 'Timeless' remained the only novel Nicholas Tchkotoua ever completed. Written in English in the mid-1940s, the plot tells the story of a young man returning to Georgia after some years away. It is no great insight to suggest that this journey of the mind was almost certainly the one he craved to make in the body. Nor does it seem a coincidence that in this imaginary pilgrimage he discovers love of the purest and most idealised kind – in the landscape where he first received it as a child. No reader can fail to be struck by the intense tone of longing and the romanticism of place that haunts this book. As the British poet Alfred Noyes noted in his forward to the original 1949 edition, it is the exquisite sorrow of distance that forms the very structure of this novel and casts such a powerful spell.

The reason for this of course, is that most of the action is based on real events. One only has to consider the bare facts of the author's life.

Prince Nicholas Tchkotoua was born in Batumi on Georgia's subtropical Black Sea coast in 1905 or 1906. The year of his birth remains slightly unclear due to the confusing array of documents carried by fleeing citizens of the new and short-lived Menshevik Georgian state (1918-1921). His father, Shalva Tchkonia, was a wealthy Georgian business-man who had married Princess Pelagie Tchkotoua – whose name Nicholas would take on after being adopted by his paternal grandfather (unlike some émigrés who created their nobility in transit). While Georgia may probably have more noble families per capita than any other country, the by then impoverished Tchkotoua line did once own an estate in the Samourzakano region of Georgia (today called Gali). Nicholas spent the first sixteen years of his life between Batumi, Tbilisi, and during the summers, Montpellier, France where his father maintained a house. The main part of his education took place at the Tbilisi Gymnasium school – and it was in the Georgian capital that his imagination was formed. When in 1918 the British army set up a garrison of 20,000 troops in Batumi, one of their ancillary workers, an English nurse called Veronica employed by the Red Cross, married the cousin of Nicholas's father. This woman – his 'aunt Veronica' as she later became known – would play a strong role in the young Georgian's future.

In 1921, as the Bolshevik army crushed the Georgian defences, the family evacuated Nicholas and he found himself back in France – the same destination as Georgia's fleeing Menshevik government. Like many émigrés, he then continued his education between Paris and Berlin until a bout of severe tuberculosis forced him to recuperate in the clean air of Switzerland. When his 'aunt' heard about his condition she then invited him to complete his convalescence in England, which he did, arriving in 1931. Staying with her in Chelsea he quickly learnt English (his fifth language) and with her encouragement then moved to the USA in 1933. After a period as a singer and performer in Hollywood, he met and married Carol Marmon, heir to the Marmon car company created by Howard Marmon – to whom the book 'Timeless' is dedicated. In 1940 Nicholas became a naturalised American citizen and the couple went on to have six children while living in Santa Barbara (where he wrote 'Timeless'), San Francisco, and Mexico. In 1954 the family moved to Europe and settled in Lausanne, Switzerland where he would maintain a home until his death there in 1984. In these later years he also lived in a number of countries – including Italy, Spain and briefly Peru.

Throughout his life Prince Tchkotoua, aided partly by his wife's wealth, was able to remain true to his Georgian aristocratic ideals, unlike many of the émigré aristocracy who ended up as waiters and taxi drivers in cities like New York and LA. As an adjunct to this he pursued his long-term interest in the diplomatic service and eventually became Ambassador for the Knights of Malta to Costa Rica, Chile, Peru and Spain where he set up embassies.

But within this colourful life one factor remained constant – a passionate and enduring interest in the land of his birth. His son Charles recalls him frequently pointing to strangers on the street remarking how they looked Georgian. He never lost his fluency in Georgian and Russian. His cousin, brought up in Soviet Tbilisi, recalls their first ever conversation in the late 1960s, taken on a phone in Bakuriani, a small resort in central Georgia. Even though by then he had been gone from Georgia for over forty five years his spoken Georgian seemed 'quite normal.'

As for his depiction of his country from afar: while it carries a slightly fairytale-like tone, for those who have visited Georgia, a country of 4.5 million sandwiched between the Greater and Lesser Caucasus, the euphoric descriptions of landscape and its people carry a ring of truth. To stand before the high Caucasus – as the main character Shota does several times – is a powerful experience. In the 19th century the sight had stopped Pushkin, Lermontov and Tolstoy in their tracks, and has inspired many pages of literature back to the day of Marco Polo. The mountains are higher and wilder than the Alps and the people living under these huge peaks had evolved their own distinctive culture and language (and script) living under the threats of avalanches, mudslides, floods and the many invading armies that surged through the passes of this strategic rocky divide between Europe from Asia. As a result Georgia possesses a disproportionately high number of dramatic hilltop castles, 12th century watchtowers, and in some remote regions the blood-feud and bride snatching may still exist (as described in the novel). Additionally the country contains high deserts, rich alluvial valleys and the world's oldest viniculture. Beyond this to the far west is its subtropical Black Sea coast (where Samourzakano is located). This had kept Georgia open to the wider world from before the time of the Greeks (Jason sailed to Colchis, the ancient name for western Georgia, to find his 'Golden Fleece'). In terms of landscape diversity alone, Georgia ranks in the world's top twelve nations – an extraordinary statistic for a country no larger than Ireland. Small wonder then that most Georgians who leave their homeland find themselves filled with nostalgia and the urge to return.

Indeed, early on in the novel the main character Shota quotes his grandfather as instructing him as a child to travel the world simply 'to be sure that there is no finer place on earth than our country.'

This, one feels, is what Nicholas Tchkotoua did, if inadvertently, for much of his life. Although he wrote 'Timeless' after a twenty-five year absence from his homeland, his memory remains sharp and less exaggerated than some may think. For instance the jousting tournaments or 'jiritoba' still do take place today, albeit in lesser forms and in high mountain villages – as in the Khevsureti region. In his time they would have been perhaps as vivid as described in the book because the Soviet relocations from the high Caucasus had yet to take place. Perhaps even more interesting is the scene in which the young Georgian prince arrives back home to discover his grandfather has disinherited him by giving away his lands to the feudal peasants. This really did happen in Georgia. A number of observers believe, and one assumes Nicholas Tchkotoua is among them, that if the same had happened across the Russian empire, the Russian Revolution would almost certainly have been averted.

One element of the plot however might need some explanation for the modern reader – the seemingly unusual reaction made by the protagonists to the diagnosis of tuberculosis. It should be noted that at the time the bulk of the novel was set (1897-1899) it would not be so strange. Then doctors still believed the illness to be hereditary and incurable – a kind of death sentence passed on through the generations. To be diagnosed with tuberculosis then would be equivalent to cancer today. Furthermore Nicholas Tchkotoua knew the disease well from his own experience. As a result his descriptions of that hinterland of consciousness are unusually powerful and may well have helped develop the novel's deeper theme of an invisible existence beyond recordable time or memory.

The discovery of this novel sitting on a shelf in a second-hand bookshop in London's Camden Town came as a great and tantalising surprise. Even now hardly any novels written by Georgians exist, let alone any available internationally. Save for a few very rare Soviet era translations and some untranslated modern novels, there is almost nothing out there to shed a clean literary light on the thought processes and emotions that make up the distinctive 'Georgian' character – from the inside.

In this vein some might make comparisons with that other celebrated love story from the Caucasus written in this period – 'Ali and Nino' by Kurban Said (the alias of the Azeri/Russian/Jewish Lev Nussimbaum). Interestingly both writers were born around the same year – 1905, both fled the Caucasus to France in 1921 from the Georgian port of Batumi. Both married American heiresses and both wrote romanticised stories of love set in their homeland in the voice of a young man close to the ages at which they left their Caucasian homelands.

But while the author of 'Ali and Nino' had been a professional writer for some years when he wrote his most famous work – set mostly in Baku, 'Timeless' came more as a gut reaction to a particular situation – set in Georgia. Prior to this book Nicholas Tchkotoua had written very little – just a few scraps of journalism. His style is far simpler and perhaps truer to the voice of a young man at that age. The young Shota's instantaneous love for his Taya is one of total and unashamed commitment.

Interestingly Georgian culture has a term for this state of full-on commitment – in the word 'guli' in Georgian ('heart' in English). It is generally believed that if actions are done with heart, they can be forgiven – even if mistaken. This book is a powerful example of this principle, indeed it is more or less spelled out in Chapter VII, 'Ishtvan Irmey,' when the Hungarian violinist declares how the only worthwhile music must be the product of a marriage of 'heart... mind and soul' playing together.

This book is written with that same Georgian 'heart' and is almost certainly about a love that really existed (there is some evidence of a real Taya in the author's life). But here one should mention a link with another very central element of Georgian culture – the cult of love as expounded by Georgia's national poet Shota Rustaveli.

This is a core element in the classical cultures of the Caucasus. Rustaveli's 12th century epic poem, 'The Knight in the Panther Skin,' is referred to several times in the text. His 1631-verse poem begins with the humble poet, Rustaveli himself, declaring an undying love for his Queen Tamara (written as Thamar in the text - see Afterword for an explanation of spellings). In 'Timeless,' Nicholas Tchkotoua's own Shota also possesses a purified and perfected devotion for his Taya. It is here that the ancient 'voice of love' is heard again – the kind bearing strong links with stories found further south in the Sufi cultures of Persia and beyond. The usual association with devotional love grows from Muslim, Arab or Hindu cultures – but Shota's love is Christian which makes it particularly interesting. There is a sense that his love is so deep it cannot possibly be merely human. In 'Timeless' the saint-like character of Father Shalva steps in to cite Rustaveli's hopeless love for his queen as an example of how the dilemmas of individual passion can be solved by placing them in the context of 'God's love.' For the modern Western reader brought up on the inheritance of Courtly Love, then 19th century Romanticism, the Sublime and the concepts of divine poetic love, it is tempting to see a link between the 12th and the 20th centuries, the Near Eastern and Western European religions in this, the elemental story of man meeting woman.

At the beginning of Chapter IV the young Shota declares, 'I loved Taya when the earth was without form and void, and darkness was upon the face of the deep. And I shall love her when it turns into a waterless, airless, frozen ball spinning aimlessly through black and dead endlessness.' Now, several decades after the author's own death and sixty years after these words were written, the description returns with a certain poignancy. Today both he and his love are physically as he described, completely without form and void. For them darkness is upon the face of the deep and the earth does spin through the airless, dead endlessness. But now the presence of their love is suddenly restored. Here in the republished pages of a book, the freshness of their feeling, the sensations and spiritual quality of a love found in those magnificent days in Tbilisi, Samourzakano and Paris do indeed return to this earth. As the author predicted with uncanny foresight, their love has taken on its own form of timelesness.

Peter Nasmyth — *September 2008*

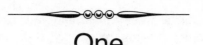

One

THE BARONESS

THAT morning the Baroness dressed more carefully than usual. She chose a black velour coat and skirt with a plain collar of sheer marquisette, which accentuated the fine lines of her handsome face and the whiteness of her carefully coiffed hair.

She was old, perhaps in her seventies, but had never conceded to Father Time anything but a numerical count of her summers and winters. She bore her age with dignity and grace, the same innate aristocratic pride which had sustained her through the trials of an eventful life.

She selected a small, almost severe black hat out of a hat box and walked to the dressing mirror. She stood before it perfectly erect and tall, adjusting the hat. Her clothes and appearance were modern, and her trim figure blended well with the room reflected in the mirror. It was a fine, warm room full of warm things from a wonderful warm past. Every article carried an aura of history: the heavy purple draperies, embroidered with gold and now faded; the massive curved bed of brown mahogany; the chairs, tables, chests; everything down to the last powder box inlaid with mother-of-pearl, spoke of a time departed.

The day outside was brilliant and young. The great city with its blooming chestnut trees, smelled of violets – as Paris would always smell as long as Paris lives. But this room was almost dark. The old Baroness treasured her privacy. Her small corner of the world was precious to her all the more so because of its smallness. The flickering sanctuary lamp in the corner cast a restless yet comforting glow on the time-honoured visage of Our Lady of Iberia – one of the icons from the faraway land where the Baroness was born. The old woman had grown to feel very secure in her presence.

Suddenly she heard quick, light footsteps outside. They paused momentarily before the door, then came a nervous staccato knock in the semi-darkness. Someone was eager to assault this citadel of the past; someone who knew that entrance would not be denied.

The Baroness recognized the footsteps and the knock. There could be but one person in the world able to invade her room at this hour, and only one person who would be welcome. Her fine face relaxed immediately, lost its immobility and aloofness; took on a softness and warmth.

"Come in, Ren," she said without turning.

The door opened slowly. The first thing that appeared was a riot of raven-black hair surrounding two sparkling eyes. Then a tall, slender, very beautiful, very excited young girl slipped inside. She wore a flowing green pyjama suit which only the very young or very handsome can wear with such a degree of ease. She shut the door quickly, leaning against it for a moment as if fearing someone might follow her.

"Granny…" she said breathlessly, throwing her hair away from her cheek with a quick sweep of her hand.

"Good morning dear," said the old lady.

"Granny… good morning. I had to talk to you… I simply had to… alone!"

She flew across the room, threw her arms around the

Baroness and buried her face in the old woman's shoulder. Only now could one appreciate the marvellous, almost uncanny resemblance between the two women separated by the barrier of at least fifty years. Every feature of the old woman's face was faithfully reproduced in the face of the girl. The same high forehead, the same prominent cheekbones, the same delicate but wilful mouth, the same large dark eyes. But only now, seeing the two together, did one realize what a regal beauty the Baroness must have been in her prime.

"Come, come, Ren," she said, stroking the girl's silky hair lovingly. "Tell me about it child."

The girl broke away from her abruptly. For a long instant she looked at the Baroness squarely.

"I am in love!"

For a second the old woman seemed taken aback. Then she rallied and returned the girl's look just as uncompromisingly.

"Are you sure, Ren?"

"Positive."

"Who is he?"

"I've not the slightest idea."

The Baroness arched her eyebrows, but without any suggestion of censure or rebuke. She simply wished to hear more.

"Have you known him long?"

"For ever."

"When did you meet him?"

"Last night."

Something resembling a wan smile crept into the corners of the old woman's faded mouth. "I'm afraid you'll have to be a little more specific Ren. That is, if you wish me to be of any help."

The girl ran her long fingers through her hair, sweeping it out of the way again.

"His name is… well, that's not important. He is a flyer, I think, and he has been in Paris only a few days. He was going to leave for the Belgian Congo at six thirty-five this morning. I'm meeting him this afternoon in the Bois. We're having dinner tonight at the Pavilion. Then we're going somewhere tonight. All this is not important Granny. The important thing is that we can't be without each other for the rest of our lives."

"Well," the Baroness said matter-of-factly, "that is pretty important isn't it."

She reached for her cane, walked across the room to an armchair and sat down, calm and imperious like a proud and dignified queen holding her court.

"Supposing we try to be rational about this, Ren? Would you like to tell me all about it… sanely?"

"Yes, yes… only to you, Granny! You'll understand!"

The girl was quick and restless. She fluttered around the room, filling every nook and cranny with her excitement. The dark hair flowing around her head looked like black silk wings. She walked from the icon corner to the dressing table and back again, touching things on the dresser as she passed with slender happy fingers. Meanwhile her words tumbled out into the air, rising and falling, shimmering with their exuberance and colour.

"There's really nothing to tell, Granny. It just happened and there's nothing anyone can do about it... You know how I detest cocktail parties… Well yesterday I had to go. I promised Beth Braganca and I couldn't disappoint her. It was the same old crowd and I had a perfectly miserable time for a while, counting seconds before I could break away. And then he came in through the door and it was all over. It was like lightning! Like spring! Like nothing else in the world!"

"Is he handsome?"

"How do I know? He's just wonderful. We stood and

looked at each other and couldn't say another word. I suppose we were too terrified at the thought that sooner or later we would have to part — that the magic would disappear and we would have to live our lives without it, eating, sleeping, and drinking cocktails with silly people. I must marry him Granny... before that happens."

"It needn't happen, Ren."

The girl stopped and looked at the old woman with hope and fright mixing in her eyes.

The Baroness rose and took hold of her cane.

"What shall I do, Granny?"

"What can you do?"

There was a brief pause. Quick quivering thoughts flashed through the girl's mind. "Well... one thing I know... I can't tell this to anyone. . . not yet. Not even to Mother. Mother has a peculiar idea that I have come into this world to live her life instead of my own."

The old Baroness knitted her brows. She tried very hard and unsuccessfully to look and feel stern.

"Your mother adores you, Ren. You're a very ungrateful child. She has had unfortunate experiences and perhaps she is inclined to be over-apprehensive..."

"Yes I know but..." cried the girl, but the Baroness cut her off with a gentle tap of her cane on the floor.

"I am still speaking, Ren, and I want you to remember my words. Love your mother Ren. Respect her. Be considerate and kind to her always. And..." she took the girl's chin and pushed it up gently, looking her straight in the eye, "...and in heaven's name don't allow her to ruin your life."

The girl suddenly embraced the old woman warmly. For many years; in fact for as long as she could remember, Ren knew she could always turn to her grandmother for sympathy, understanding and a reliably sober dose of wisdom in every crisis of her restless childhood. She loved her grandmother more than anyone else. But it was something greater than love. More a kind of communion of spirit; a genuine inner connection between two women.

"Very well, Ren," said the old woman with a reserved tenderness that never threatened sentimentality. "Run along and stop tormenting yourself. God knows what he is doing. I am going out for my walk and I may be a little late in getting back. There!"

She kissed the girl's forehead and the audience was over. Ren slipped out of the room as quickly as she had entered. Her feet seemed not to touch the floor, as if lifted from its surface by her own blinding state of happiness.

Left alone the Baroness stood motionless for a few moments. Her proud face seemed frozen. Whatever thoughts that may have troubled her, produced no disturbance whatsoever on her calm exterior. They kept themselves well submerged within the deeper layers of her soul. Then slowly she walked to the door and turned the key in the lock. A needless precaution because no one except Ren would ever dare disturb the sanctity of her private world. Yet the Baroness always felt more secure and comforted with the thin strip of iron set between herself and the rest of the house.

She walked back to the corner of the room where the flickering tongue of the sanctuary lamp sent dancing shadows across the wallpaper, and knelt down. Although an intensely religious woman, her faith had never been ruled by dogmatic commandments or restraints. She prayed whenever she felt the urge for an intimate communion with her God. But this morning the urge was instantaneous and overpowering.

She left the house some fifteen minutes later, walking with her usual measured and unhurried step. Her erect posture belied her age, because but for the cane, from a distance one could have easily mistaken her for a young woman out for an early morning tryst with the man of her heart.

The old gardener trimming the hedge in front of the mansion took off his hat. His wrinkled weather-bitten face contracted into a baked-apple smile.

"Bonjour, Madame la Baronne."

"Bonjour, Emil."

The old Baroness was not particularly liked within her own circle, being generally considered too distant and strict. But the people she encountered during her daily routine loved her for her evenness of manner – given without a shade of familiarity or haughtiness. Newsboys, policemen, street vendors, and the gatekeepers to the fine mansions lining this exclusive street, had known her for many years and never missed greeting her warmly but respectfully during her daily walks.

The day was crisp and cloudless. The sky, the air, the pavements, the trees, and even the grey smoke curling from the chimneys, seemed to be moulded out of a transparent blue glass. Every element varied in intensity, the sky appeared the bluest, the pavement the dullest, but even the pavement possessed its own subtle shade of sapphire. On a morning such as this all living things feel a touch of immortality. Small wonder then that the sparrows dancing in the gutter dust chirped out a defiant message and refused to show any fear to the tall woman walking past.

But the Baroness seemed not to notice the blueness of the day nor the birds at her feet. She walked on without any undue haste or pauses, looking straight ahead. She entered the park, almost deserted at this early hour, but instead of sitting down on a bench near the fountain as had been her routine for many years, she continued on, much to the disappointment of lovesick pigeons that normally swarmed around her feet in anticipation of her customary largesse.

She continued for the entire length of the park then stepped out into a narrow street on the far side. This neighbourhood was rather more modest and obviously beyond the borders of her realm, for she received no more greetings or smiles. No one seemed to know the old Baroness here. It felt like a different world, foreign, distant, almost hostile.

She crossed a traffic-jammed boulevard and walked along a quiet and lonely street lined with maples and lindens. She turned one corner, then another, until finally arriving at the tall grille fence of a small and antiquated cemetery. The fence was broken and twisted in many places, as well as being almost completely overgrown with ivy and vines. The main entrance faced the Boulevard on the far side, but the Baroness shunned this entrance. Instead she entered the hallowed ground through a narrow gate off to the side. Immediately she found herself enveloped by a deep sense of serenity – that essential quality of any burial ground. Around her birds fluttered in the tall cypresses or basked in the golden-blue sunshine. Zinnias, lilies and marigolds embraced the marble slabs inscribed with the names of those who had once enjoyed days exactly such as this.

Two gravediggers in sweat-spotted blue overalls stood chest-deep in a freshly dug grave, arguing spiritedly about a political candidate up for re-election the next week. As soon as they noticed the approaching old lady they stopped their argument and picked up their shovels again. Immediately spadefulls of black earth started flying out of the hole with a startling rapidity.

"Do you men know where Prince d'Iberio is to be buried this morning?" asked the Baroness.

The workmen put down their shovels, removed their caps and scratched their scrawny necks.

"All sorts of people get buried in this place Madame," one of them finally ventured, then added a touch of homespun philosophy. "But by the time they reach this piece of earth their names don't mean much any more."

"Then you don't know?" the Baroness said curtly. She was in no mood for banter this morning.

"Wait," said the other man. "Could your man be the gentleman who's moving into that elegant spot near the Basilica? If he is you'd better hurry, Madame. The procession came through the main gate half an hour ago."

"You can hear them singing," said the first man.

True enough, the faint sounds of a choral melody could be heard in the distance. No words were distinguishable but the Baroness recognized the ancient lament of 'De Profundis.'

She thanked the men and walked on, guided by the sounds of singing. The monuments and tombstones grew bigger and more imposing as she approached the Basilica – the section of the cemetery reserved for the rich and prominent. Soon she started to catch snatches of the antiphon:

"Apud Dominum misericordia et copiosa apud Eum redemptio...."

She turned away from the main alley then saw a neat crowd of people, sombre and darkly dressed, standing in a wide semicircle round an open grave.

A distinguished-looking gathering in which the men wore morning coats and striped trousers, holding top-hats in their hands. The women wore dark dresses or black skirts and coats. The relatives of the dead man stood in a small, grief-stricken group aside from the others – obviously his sons and daughters, with their children beside them looking nervous and bewildered by the mystery of death which they were too young to understand. Among this younger group one man immediately attracted the Baroness's attention. Tall and very handsome in a dark, Mediterranean way, his sensitive face and entire figure bore the signs of profound sorrow. He alone among the young stood out as the one suffering the severest blow. That would be Prince Theimuraz, the Baroness thought, the favourite grandson of the departed patriarch.

The Baroness chose not to join the crowd of mourners. Instead she stood some distance away as just another figure among those attracted to the spectacle of such a stately funeral; the chance visitors to the cemetery, the street hawkers who had just followed the procession in, the newspaper reporters, cemetery employees and men from the undertakers.

The young priest read his prayer with great feeling.

"Enter not into judgment with Thy servant, Oh Lord; for in Thy sight shall no man be justified unless through Thee he find pardon for all his sins…"

But the Baroness never followed the words. Her face registered no emotion whatsoever, neither grief nor interest in the service, or the people standing nearby. She presented a completely detached face, a physical shell with all evidence of her spiritual and emotional state invisible. If she felt sorrow, it was of such completeness and profundity it left no room for the usual expressions of bereavement.

"…who, whilst he was living, was marked with the sign of the Holy Trinity, who livest and reignest, world without end. Amen."

The short service was drawing to a close. The casket was lowered into the grave, blessed, then hard lumps of soil started drumming against its silver lid. Gradually the relatives and friends broke away into smaller groups talking in low voices. Out in the street the chauffeurs of the limousines ended their conversations and returned to their cars. A weeping woman, one of the dead man's daughters, was helped out of the cemetery by her sons and the crowd of onlookers steadily melted away. Soon life once again reigned supreme among the living.

The priest and the choir then departed, which served as the signal for the final exodus. Within a few minutes the crowd had completely disappeared. A few cemetery attendants remained to arrange the mountain of flowers on the fresh grave and three men from a stone-cutters' office diligently measured the space to be occupied by a Carrara marble monument.

Suddenly the Baroness discovered she stood quite alone on the neatly clipped lawn. She looked around and realising that all the mourners were now gone, slowly walked over to the graveside. She stopped a few feet from the edge and gazed down on the freshly turned sod and satin flower-ribbons that bore all the conventional inscriptions and condolences. She noticed several written in a strange and ancient-looking Georgian script, but these the Baroness could not read.

She stood motionless for a long time, quite oblivious to the vigour and energy of the natural world surrounding her. It could have been for a few minutes or an hour. When she finally regained her sense of time and place the cemetery attendants and stonecutters were gone. Peace and tranquility had returned once again.

Suddenly she heard someone speak her name from near by, almost in a whisper.

Casting a quick sidelong glance she saw a man was now standing close beside her. Slowly she turned her head and recognized him instantly – the young man she had noticed earlier on in the crowd. He stood even taller than she first judged, and also thinner. He wore a plain black suit, a black tie and a crêpe band on his sleeve. The lines of sorrow on his face still betrayed the depth of his grief.

The eyes of the Baroness wandered from the crêpe band down to his hand, and noticed he held a square, flattish object, carefully wrapped in paper.

"Did you speak to me?" asked the Baroness.

The young man appeared suddenly awkward. "Yes," he replied in a low voice. "I have something for you Madame."

He indicated at the parcel in his hand. The Baroness leaned heavily on her cane, trying to gather her thoughts.

"What is it?"

"It is something left by my grandfather," answered the young man. "He knew you would come. He said … well, he asked me to give this to you."

The Baroness stared at the young man, and noticing he seemed to have grown paler, thought to herself, 'his eyes... his face... his figure... his manner... everything!'

A warm lump formed in her throat and momentarily choked her into speechlessness.

"Please, Madame… Grandfather had spoken to me about you before he… died. He wanted you to have this… He asked me to…" His voice broke off as he struggled with his emotions. "I am very sorry to have disturbed you… Please forgive me."

The Baroness took the package with her long fingers which suddenly tightened around the soft paper with an almost desperate grip. For the first time in many years her eyes became moist, despite all her attempts to fight back this display of feeling. "You are very kind…," she managed to say slowly. "You are very, very kind..."

"A pleasure, Madame," muttered the young man, also clearly struggling for words. "A pleasure…"

He too was scanning her face, examining it minutely, hesitating to break off this brief meeting. The Baroness suddenly feared the young man would ask her more questions, and was greatly relieved to see that, the moment he saw her become conscious of his gaze, he lowered his eyes. This meant there would be none.

"Good-bye, Madame."

"Good-bye, and thank you again."

That was all. She turned and walked hurriedly away, as though afraid someone might run up behind and deprive her of this new and most treasured possession. She walked faster and faster, clasping the parcel in her hand until she found herself back on the city street, comfortingly lost in the mid-morning crowd. She paused, drew in a deep breath, then stood still on the pavement not daring to move lest she and her priceless parcel draw anyone's attention. She did not know whose attention but felt that no power in the world must be allowed to separate her from the paper-wrapped object now clasped in her hand.

When a dilapidated cab drew up to the curbside and the driver said, "Taxi, Madame?" she never hesitated. Once inside the shabby little fortress on wheels she felt isolated from the world outside and suddenly safe with her treasure. A glorious feeling.

"Where to, Madame?" asked the driver.

Where to...? Home...? No. Somehow the very thought of home disturbed her at this moment. Home was a place which she shared with others, no matter how remotely, and she did not want to share her mood with anyone. She wanted to be left alone with it, to nurse it, and to enjoy its poignant bitterness in the privacy of her own soul. No, not home.

"Where to?" repeated the driver.

"Café de la Colombe," she said suddenly.

The driver blinked his watery eyes. This he did not expect at such an hour, and from such an elegant white-haired lady who had obviously just left the cemetery.

"Pardon?" he said.

"Café de la Colombe," repeated the Baroness.

The driver shrugged and revved up the motor. What did he care? It was a long fare and business had been slow this morning. He shifted the gears and the ancient contraption lurched forward with a sudden screeching of its tyres. For the first time since leaving the cemetery the Baroness felt completely relaxed. The lines of strain on her handsome face gave way to her more usual calm and aloof expression; the one familiar to all who knew her well.

The famous café was almost deserted at this hour. Too early both for the tourists and also the Parisians, who rarely showed up before aperitif hour. Just a few young couples sat around enjoying their morning coffee, croissants and each other. The smiling maitre-d'hôtel met the Baroness with a bow and an inquisitive curve of his eyebrows.

"This way, Madame…?"

With a professional sweep of his hand he indicated the tables on the pavement – usually much sought after by out-of-town visitors who wished to absorb the atmosphere of the Parisian street. But the Baroness had other plans.

"I wish to go upstairs," she said.

"Upstairs, Madame? Very few guests go there before the luncheon hour. You may be quite lonely there, Madame."

"Can I go?"

"But of course Madame. This way please."

The Baroness knew the way. The empty room upstairs spread before her like a desert of chequered tablecloths and sparkling silverware. A lonely waiter, sleepy as an autumn fly, stood in the corner, napkin draped over his arm. The Baroness stopped still in the doorway sweeping the room with her eyes until finally spotting what she wanted. She walked unhurriedly over to a secluded corner near the window and sat in the chair pulled out by the maitre-d'hôtel. He then left, turning the Baroness over to the sleepy waiter.

"Bring me a cup of coffee with milk, garçon," she said simply. "And then I do not wish to be disturbed."

Now at last the Baroness was alone, miles away from anyone who liked or disliked her. She sat in her chair, straight and immobile, gazing through the window at the streamers of fleecy clouds which had now appeared in the sky. They floated majestically across the blue nothingness just as they had floated for millions of years, and would float for millions of years to come.

Presently the coffee arrived and the waiter departed to his somnolent corner.

But the Baroness never touched the steaming cup. Instead she placed her package carefully on the tabletop as a nervous and irresistible excitement began rising up inside her. She felt it ebb and flow through her body like the surge and recoil of surf.

With trembling hands she started to unwrap the parcel. Several sheets of meticulously folded paper encircled it. She noticed how the creases had worn through in places. Clearly they had been created a good many years ago.

Finally, with the last layer removed, the Baroness looked down on a thick stack of paper. She separated the now yellowing sheets with her fingers and suddenly realised that she held a manuscript, written in a precise and orderly hand.

The first sheet of paper bore the title, a single word written in English,

"TIMELESS"

A strange, non-committal title that seemed almost suspended in the air. But the Baroness read it through many times as if it carried some deeply hidden meaning. Then she turned over the first sheet.

The page was blank save for a short dedication written in the top right-hand corner:

"To the One I have lost once, to have forever."

The Baroness contemplated these words for some minutes. Then the beautiful city beyond the window, the deserted room of the celebrated café, the chequered tablecloths, in fact everything, slowly dissolved before her eyes.

She turned the page and began to read:

Two

GRANDFATHER

BEFORE I went to Switzerland as a very young boy, my grandfather told me:

"This is your home. Whenever you are ready to come back it will be waiting for you – be it six months or six hundred years. Don't hurry. Take a good look at the world. I want you to be sure there is no finer place on the face of the earth than our country."

My grandfather was right. I knew it when I came back twelve years later for a brief summer visit. It is hard to describe the loveliness of this remotest corner of Europe, especially in spring or summer.

Broad green valleys covered with vineyards; park-like meadows, orchards, tea plantations and subtropical forests cut by snow-fed rivers… Then picturesque towns, monasteries and feudal castles set like fortresses on sheer cliffs; all remnants of a heroic era when this land stood as a Christian bulwark against the Moslem foe. To the west orange groves can be found by the sea and to the north, Europe's most formidable mountain range. This icy wilderness of broken granite and perennial snow has still, over many centuries, only permitted two passes to be cut through. The home of a simple and proud people for whom the touch of the sword handle is still the most comforting feeling they know.

It was my country.

I belonged here. I knew it the moment I set foot in Batoum after a long sea voyage from Marseilles – which partly retraced the route of the Argonauts in their quest for the Golden Fleece. And this feeling grew with each new panorama unfurling majestically outside my railway compartment window.

Tick-a-tack, tick-a-tack, tick-a-tack.

My country was singing me its welcome with the clatter of iron wheels. The song brought me closer and closer to my home; to the only one I had loved since early childhood.

I had never known my parents. My mother died when I was too young to remember. My father fell just a few months later, crossing the snow-swept Balkan passes with the Czar's army on its futile journey toward Constantinople.

Tick-a-tack, tick-a-tack, tick-a-tack.

Railroad travel on the Batoum-Tiflis line, completed just a few years earlier in 1883, was surprisingly comfortable. However its greatest virtue has to be the abundance of truly magnificent scenery constantly presented to the traveller. Nowhere in the world, not even in the Swiss Alps, is nature on so bountiful display as in the ancient lands of Colchis and Iberia – which, when combined, compose today's kingdom of Georgia.

We arrived at Tiflis (or Tbilisi if you prefer the local name) toward evening. The town, elegantly located on the Kura river (or Mtkvari as it called in Georgian) and against the purple backdrop of the Trialet mountains, now it rose like a sudden mirage outside my window. The imposing stone vision of its fortress bathed sweetly in the last rays of the setting sun. A truly memorable sight.

Tiflis was founded by the Georgian King Vakhtang early in the fifth century. Legend has it that one day while the king hunted on the banks of the Kura, he shot and wounded a stag. The animal however quickly jumped into a hot sulphur spring, bathed its wound and disappeared off into a thicket. The health-giving properties of the sulphur waters so impressed the king that he immediately decided to build a town there naming it Tbilisi, which literally means 'hot springs.'

The history of the town closely parallels the history of Georgia. Razed to the ground many times by Turks, Persians and Mongols (Tamerlane alone assaulted and demolished it eight times), Tiflis rose again after every catastrophe. It remained Georgia's capital and cultural centre until the turn of the nineteenth century when the Russian Czars finally took over the protection of the small Christian nation – at that time bleeding to death under the relentless blows of Islam.

Now Tiflis flourished once again, at long last enjoying genuine peace and security. The newest areas of the town presented a thoroughly modern air, with imposing public buildings, fine churches, splendid mansions, broad avenues and handsome parks. Set at the vital crossroads between Europe and Asia, the city attracted trade from every part of the two continents. As a result the Tiflis markets rank among the world's finest.

As the administrative centre of the Caucasus and residence of the Viceroy, Tiflis is a cosmopolitan metropolis. Its balmy climate and beautiful scenery has drawn many prominent and wealthy residents, not only from the Caucasus but Russia as well. Many, like my grandfather, established and maintained homes there.

A carriage sent by Grandfather met me at the station and took me directly to his house – the same I had left twelve years earlier. I stood staring up at the large mansion built of white stone with its wide stairway and ancient coat-of-arms set over the entrance. Suddenly a liveried, medal-wearing doorman – the one I had known since my childhood – swung open the heavy door in a triumphant gesture. This old man had been in Grandfather's service all his life and originally came from Grandfather's feudal fief in Samourzakani, western Georgia.

He then handed me over to another servant, a taciturn man called Erast whom I had never seen before. He wore the traditional Georgian costume, complete with cartridge cases across his chest and a dagger attached to his belt. He too came from Grandfather's estate and spoke only Georgian. The language is an ancient, highly developed tongue with mysterious origins and its own characteristic alphabet dating from the eighth century B.C. – which I discovered I had somewhat forgotten during my long sojourn abroad.

After I had been escorted to my room I tried to dismiss Erast, but Erast would not be dismissed. Assigned as my personal valet, he seemed to have orders to wait on me hand and foot whether I liked it or not. I begged him not to plague my every step, but to no avail. He knew his duties and he would perform them to the letter.

"I am your man," he repeated stoically.

Finally I gave up and started to unpack my things with Erast hovering over me constantly.

I expected Grandfather to summon me downstairs to meet him, but when he didn't I took a bath then changed my clothes. Erast played a silent but active part in both.

Afterwards, Erast suddenly announced

"The Prince is waiting for you in his study."

"Why didn't you tell me before?" I asked annoyed.

"There was no hurry," Erast answered dispassionately. "The Prince is in his study all day."

I almost ran downstairs with Erast close at my heels.

It was with some anxiety that I approached the massive oak door which I knew so well. I tried to brace myself for a shock – it is not easy meeting someone you love after a gap of many years.

It has been six years since I last saw my grandfather. On that occasion he visited me in Switzerland and had appeared in vigorous good health for his age. But six years is a long time for anyone and he could have aged considerably. To see this would have been a cruel blow, for I had grown very fond of my image of Grandfather, carried with me unchanged throughout the years of separation.

"The Prince is in the study," said Erast, noticing my hesitation.

I gave him a sharp look and knocked.

There was no answer.

I knocked again, louder.

"Come in!" said a firm voice.

That voice has not changed, I thought happily, still just as I remembered it – deep, warm and resonant. Indeed legend had it that during battle Grandfather had never needed any messengers, always relying on his booming voice to carry orders directly to the command.

I stepped inside to find the same wonderful room I remembered from childhood. In those days it had always filled me with awe. I'd experienced the room as a thrilling, mysterious world of countless books set in yellow calfskin covers, and dark brown leather divans so big and cool you seemed to plunge into the sea every time you sat down. The walls were covered with weapons and hunting trophies, as well as rare and historic photographs. One photograph in particular had always impressed me. It showed my grandfather standing next to Emperor Alexander III. Despite the heroic stature of the peace-loving Czar, my grandfather stood taller. As a child this had always been a source of intense pride.

The picture was still there and Grandfather was still taller than the Emperor.

"Gamarjoba!" said Grandfather.

Although educated in Paris, Bologna and Jena; known as a scholar, traveller and linguist with skills sufficient to leave him at home anywhere in the world, he had remained as Georgian as the sulphur springs of Tiflis. He stood up from behind the desk to his full height. I was delighted to see him hardly aged at all since the day we parted. The same bright blue eyes of a feudal romantic – or so I had categorised him then – glowed back warmly from under his bushy eyebrows. His face wore that same long curling moustache, now almost white, and underneath it the same smile. Over his body he bore a beautiful green kouladja – our medieval court dress – which he preferred at home to the gold-braided uniform of a retired General of the Imperial Cavalry.

"Gamarjoba, Shota!"

Once again the unusual meaning of this salutation struck me as perhaps the best indicator of the Georgian national character, and a fine example of how a people's psychology grows out of its history.

"May victory be yours…"

In this way princes and peasants, landlords and mountain brigands, merchants and artisans, greet each other every morning. The correct answer is 'Gagimarjos' – 'May victory be yours too.' I had always thought this far more than mere custom. In the securer countries of Western Europe, daily salutations usually referred to matters of business and material welfare. Russians wish each other 'gentle health.' Frugal Chinese inquire 'Have you eaten well today?' But not the Georgians. They have been taught by a cruel history that to enjoy work, food, health and indeed life, first one must possess victory; a victory against an ever-present and merciless foe.

"May victory be yours!"

"Gagimarjos!"

I kissed Grandfather's shoulder as was the custom. He kissed my forehead and almost drowned me in the soft whiskers of his moustache. It was a fine feeling; more precious than any caress in the world.

I was home.

His powerful arm wrapped around my shoulders and he pressed me to his side with a restrained tenderness. Then he pushed me away and held me at arm's length, scrutinizing me with a pair of shining blue eyes.

"You're big, Shota.... You've grown up to be a fine strong man..," he said with great satisfaction, "...just like your father."

He laughed with a sound like distant thunder. It rumbled and rolled as his teeth sparkled like polished ivory.

"Stay where you are boy. Let me take a good look at you."

Grandfather resumed his place behind an enormous polished desk, its surface piled high with antique books and documents. He had been working on a comprehensive history of our country, starting with Kartlos, the great-grandson of Noah who settled here in the twentieth century B.C. to found the race of Kartvelians, the first Georgians.

This monumental work had taken up the last twenty years of his life. It often inspired famous European archaeologists, historians and anthropologists to visit Tiflis and confer with Grandfather. I could see he still remained deeply engaged with his grand task.

I continued standing in the middle of the room feeling embarrassed as Grandfather studied me as he would an interesting museum piece.

"Turn around," he said finally.

I did.

"You're tall enough," he observed calmly, "but thin. They must have fed you poorly in Switzerland."

"No, Grandfather," I said, "they took excellent care of me."

"Hrrumph," said Grandfather and jerked his great moustache up and down – the usual sign he was thinking.

There followed a brief pause.

"Do you believe in God?"

"Yes sir," I said.

"In Our Lord Jesus Christ and the Holy Trinity?"

"Yes sir."

"Hrrumph," said Grandfather obviously satisfied with my answers. "Do you ride well?"

"Fairly well," I said. "I rode at school every day."

"Shoot?"

"Yes sir. They had a rifle range in the village."

The tips of the white moustache lifted defiantly. "That's no good. A young man must be at home in the saddle and a dead shot with a rifle. Do you know how they teach boys in our mountains?"

"No, Grandfather."

"As soon as a boy is strong enough to carry a gun he is trained. Then they give him three cartridges and send him out into the forest. If he comes back with three killed animals, he's a man and gets a horn of wine. But if he wastes even one shot he has failed."

"I'm afraid I wouldn't pass that test, Grandfather. They do things differently over there."

"I know," nodded Grandfather smiling. "That's why I'm glad to see you home. You won't get any Proudhon or Marx here, but we'll take good care of you otherwise. Now let me hear your French."

He leaned back in his chair and shut his eyes. For a moment I stood there confused, then guessing what he might want I recited a short French poem.

"Not bad," said Grandfather without opening his eyes. "Now give me something in English."

After a second's hesitation I went into 'To be or not to be' but Grandfather stopped me twice to correct my pronunciation. I was amazed to discover he knew the soliloquy by heart. I'd no idea he knew English so well. The longer one knew Grandfather the more astonished one grew at his versatility of knowledge. He seemed fully conversant in almost every subject you raised.

"All right," he said finally, interrupting my recital. "Now sit down and let's discuss other matters."

I sat on the edge of one of the big divans while Grandfather stroked his moustache and cleared his throat.

"Are you glad to be at home?"

"Yes sir, very," I said.

"Were you surprised when I asked you to come?"

"I was very happy."

Grandfather knitted his bushy eyebrows. "I asked you to come because I wanted to speak to you, and because your doctors have advised that your health was much better and you could stand the trip without any ill effects."

"Yes," I said quickly, "I've been feeling very well of late... very well."

"Thank God," said Grandfather with deep feeling. "You don't know what it means to me. It makes me the happiest man in the world to see you strong and well."

Yes, at this moment Grandfather was happy. He always betrayed his happiness by switching into French, often in mid sentence. French had always been his 'happy language,' ever since his Sorbonne days. He spoke it beautifully, with that rare and flexible finesse of a Louis XIV aristocrat. Even today this same elegance of address is still highly regarded among the better French-speaking circles. Listening to him I began to feel ashamed of my own Lamartine rendition, creditable as it may have seemed.

"Thank you, Grandfather," I said.

He extracted a curved Turkish pipe from the drawer and proceeded to fill it with a finely cut tobacco from a brass humidor.

"Shota," he said striking a match and inhaling the first whiff of aromatic smoke, "have you ever thought of your future?"

"Yes sir," I said.

"Have you any idea what you would like to do?"

"Yes sir."

"Let me hear it."

This was a difficult moment. All the men in our family since the dawn of our country's history had been soldiers. They fought during the Roman invasion; they had battled Turks, Arabs, Mongols and Persians. They had taken part in the Crusades and later served under the banners of the Czars. To deviate from this age-old tradition would be an unheard-of radicalism; almost a sacrilege.

"I thought that my education fitted me rather well for a diplomatic career," I said.

A dense cloud of tobacco smoke enveloped Grandfather's face for a moment. But when it cleared I saw he remained as calm as before.

"The diplomatic service, eh?" he said.

"Yes sir," I replied.

"I've never thought much of diplomats," he said. "It is a peculiar calling, admirably suited to homeless French émigrés and Baltic barons; or those who like to knock around the world bargaining, flattering and lying like the Persian merchants in Tiflis Maidan. But then... I'm an old-fashioned soldier I suppose. I've always felt that the Czar doesn't need advocates, only loyal soldiers. You know his reign started with a bad omen? Did you hear about that catastrophe on Khadynka field in Moscow during the coronation?"

"Yes sir," I said meekly.

"Thousands of people were trampled to death by stamped-ing crowds. That means only one thing… his rule will be a difficult one. He'll need every loyal man he can get!"

There was sadness in his voice and I felt almost sorry for him. To me, reared in the tradition of Western liberalism, his views appeared a little strange and foreign. However I could not help respecting, even admiring them, just as I had always respected and admired him. I knew his views would also contain the same qualities of generosity, loyalty, honesty and tolerance. I had always been fascinated by Grandfather's seeming paradoxical ability to mix the most advanced learning with what I had considered until then, a feudal romanticism.

"Of course if you feel that way about it, Grandfather…" I began, but he interrupted me.

"No," he said firmly. "I've no right to influence you. Your life is yours to live and suffer. You're responsible to God for it and no one else. If you want to be a diplomat, you will be a diplomat. When the time comes, and if I am still alive, I will go to St. Petersburg and speak to the young Czar about you. Last year at the coronation he asked me to see him personally whenever I wanted anything."

I was deeply touched by his attitude. "Thank you sir," I said.

For a few moments Grandfather sat smoking and thinking. I instinctively felt that the question of my future career was not the only reason for my being summoned to Tiflis, in fact not even the main reason. Something else was on Grandfather's mind, something that bothered him, that he wished to discuss with me.

I was right.

"Shota," he said finally, knocking ashes out of his dying pipe, "in a few days we'll go to Samourzakani. I want you to see the place which will be your home, whether you live there or not, for the rest of your life."

"I'll be glad to come," I said eagerly.

I had been in Samourzakani before, but only as a child. My recollections remained intensely romanticised: a sombre castle built centuries ago; an ancient monastery on a hill; a swift-swirling river; dark forbidding mountains with neatly constructed villages clinging to their sides. Yes, I very much wanted to visit Samourzakani again, to meet the people who lived there and tilled its rich earth for so many generations.

"You will see Vano Maradze again, a good and honest man," Grandfather continued more pensively. "He will be very happy to see you after so many years – his future master."

The Maradzes had been managers of our family estate since the days of Queen Thamar – which means from the twelfth century. They had grown to be as much a part of the property as its mountains and river. Things change slowly in rural Georgia. In very few other parts of the world have traditions held so powerful a grip on the people as in our land. Nowhere is the past such an integral part of the present as here.

I thought I detected the sparkle of laughter in Grandfather's eyes.

"Vano Maradze will probably tell you I am a madman. He has been terribly unhappy with me for the past six years."

The sparkle disappeared and his eyes became serious.

"He has good reason to think that I am slightly unbalanced, Shota. But if I know you understand me, we can handle him."

"I will, Grandfather," I said.

"Six years ago after I saw you in Switzerland, I went to Samourzakani on a routine visit. I called the people together and told them to take over the land lying idle and work it. I gave them my word that as long as I lived no one would challenge their right to the fruits of their free labour, or demand back any portion of it. Vano Maradze almost cried when he heard this. He begged me to reconsider; to take the land back from them. Instead, within a few months I did the same again in other villages on our estate. I gave away the lands... vineyards, pastures, fields and forests which our forefathers had gathered together over twelve hundred years."

He pulled out a document from a drawer in his desk.

"Here is a short inventory of the lands and properties which I assigned to our peasants, along with their names."

Then placing the document to one side he took a beautifully bound book from among the many standing on his desk, then laid it out in front of him. He stroked the surface as if it were something alive and precious, then opened it.

"Listen to these words of Roustavelli, Shota."

'Things that you take and keep are lost to you for ever; things that you give away are for ever yours.'

"I have read a good many books, great and profound, but never encountered any truer or wiser words. Because in fact no man is richer than his neighbour, nor happier than the man across the street. The only way to achieve happiness is to spread happiness. The only way to gain wealth is to share it. Unless our greedy world in its drunken urge for power learns this truth, it will drown in its own blood and tears."

He closed the book and placed it back on the desk.

I listened captivated. I had known of Grandfather's great generosity, but this was more than generosity. This was the unswerving will of a man inspired to live up to his own lofty ideals.

He spoke in a low voice without any drama or overemphasis, yet every one of his words burned into my soul.

"For many years I have been working with broken bits of stone. Here they are..." He gestured toward several archaeological specimens on the desk. "...the remnants of once proud civilizations. Men bled for these stones. They toiled and suffered to create something they thought would prove eternal and indestructible. They held great faith in granite, mortar and the skill of their artisans. They set out to defeat time feeling certain they had succeeded. But today these small pieces of broken stone are already hard to find. In a few hundred years they will disappear without trace."

Grandfather spoke with deep conviction. Clearly he had given the subject much thought and his words made a powerful impression.

"Man is building another stone and granite mirage today. It is rising toward the sky ready to envelop the entire world. I have read Karl Marx – a book condemning human greed. A thoroughly futile book because it attempts to fight fire with fire, greed with greed, violence with violence. It condemns material oppression while holding up materialism as the only antidote."

He smiled for a second. "Our fine and honest Vano Maradze would understand it. True, he would condemn it as a malicious and dangerous creed. He would try to fight it with violence and oppression. But he would never understand that it is only possible to fight the element of time – or the essence of materialism – with timeless, intangible weapons.

"Never trust time, Shota, or anything that it touches. It is the most fleeting of all mirages because with every tick of the clock it turns today into tomorrow, leaves behind nothing but bitterness and regret. Seek happiness in timelessness and wealth in eternal truth. When you come to Samourzakani you'll be the poorest d'Iberio who has ever come there – and the very richest. Furthermore, you will never need Vano Maradze and his armed men to guard your riches. They are now in the hands of a far better keeper, and He will see you through to the kind of happiness that is indeed timeless.

"I am getting on in years and who knows how soon God may wish to summon me…"

After a brief pause Grandfather continued.

"Those people there have nothing but my word to show for their rights and you are not bound by my word, Shota. Strictly speaking my actions were high-handed and illegal – according to man's law – and you would be fully within your legal rights to take the land away from them, or charge rent for its use. It is your land, Shota, and I want you to decide for yourself, without considering my feelings. What do you say to the proposition?"

"I am proud of you, Grandfather," I said with great feeling and I saw his face instantly light up. "I want to be bound by your word if you care to hand it down to me. And in turn I promise to hand it down to my children."

He rose, walked over to me and embraced me warmly and passionately. "You're giving me the greatest happiness any man can hope for, Shota – the right to complete my earthly wanderings without regrets or fear."

He broke away from me and walked back to the desk. His every movement reflected his obvious joy, as if finally relieved of a burden carried for many years. Then he approached me again and put his arm around my shoulder. "Come on," he said, "dinner is waiting. It is said 'Give your guests food first, and the pleasant words after…'"

We walked to the door. I was still too overcome by Grandfather's passionate declaration to make any reply. Besides, it was wonderful to see him in such an exuberant mood – clearly that of a thoroughly happy man.

Three

TAYA

IT happened some days after my arrival in Tiflis.

The day started just like any other. The sky lay over the city as a canopy of blue silk skillfully embroidered here and there with flecks of high white cloud. My room on the second floor of Grandfather's house was flooded with golden sunshine, so thick it seemed to ring out as it hit the hardwood floor.

That day was superb and bore no omen of any kind, beginning for me in more or less the usual way. The excitement of being in Tiflis with my grandfather still dominated my time. I had written letters to nearly everyone I knew in Switzerland and France, and browsed extensively through Grandfather's library.

I sat down to write a letter to Dr. Bauer. Before leaving Davos I had promised to report on my health to him at least once a week. Erast stood hovering over me like the angel of death.

"Erast!" I said finally, putting down the pen. "I can't write with someone looking over my shoulder."

"I don't read," Erast said bluntly.

"I know you don't, not French anyway. But your looking over my shoulder makes me nervous. Please don't do it."

Erast sounded slightly hurt. "I will look out the window."

"Couldn't you go somewhere else," I said, "just for a while and leave me alone?"

Erast looked at the sky and twitched his black moustache. He was not given to hasty response and weighed my words carefully.

"No," he said at length.

"No? Why?" I demanded.

"I promised Prince Didi Platon."

'Didi' translates literally as 'big' in our language, but it implies more than that; rather a kind of deep and affectionate respect. I had not heard Grandfather called "Didi" since the death of my old nurse Nino. She had come with me to Switzerland, only to die there of sheer homesickness a few years later. She could never adapt to the comfortable and easy life so far away from her native mountains. But she would not leave me because, according to tradition, a nurse remained with her charge for life. She would always say 'Didi' when speaking of Grandfather and I confess I found it heartening to hear again.

"What did you promise Prince Platon?"

Erast contemplated the question for a long time. "I promised him to take care of you."

"All right," I said, "so you did. But surely he did not mean that you hang around the way you do."

"I gave Prince Didi Platon my word."

It was senseless to argue because Erast's determination was not of the usual kind. Once he had declared his position, he would not surrender it under any circumstance. But still I made one last attempt:

"Don't you know anyone here in Tiflis? A girl perhaps?"

Erast lowered his eyes. "Yes, Master."

A ray of hope…

"Why don't you go and visit her, Erast? Here, I'll give you some money. Take her out, buy her some earrings… or sweet things. Here, Erast! Here are five roubles."

Erast looked at the money in my hand and shook his head. "No," he said, "I promised Prince Didi Platon. No one can release me from my promise but Prince Didi Platon."

I gave up.

We were interrupted by a brief knock on the door and Grandfather entered the room. He wore his uniform of the 17th Dragoons, the regiment he commanded during the war of 1877, and he wore it proudly. It added a strange youthfulness to all his movements and a dashing air to his already distinguished presence.

"Good morning, Shota," he said, giving me a sturdy hug. He smelt of sun and fresh air so I knew he had just returned to the house from outside. "We are having lunch in the big dining room today. I have just collected a superb archaeological relic from the station and I need you to take a good look at it."

He laughed and suddenly even Erast lost all his annoying qualities, becoming almost pleasant. There was something about Grandfather's personality that could instantly dispel all one's misgivings and drive every hint of gloom from a room.

"Then later in the afternoon we are going to Countess Gedeminoff's garden party. It's a social highlight of the summer season here. I promised to bring you."

This I found slightly disturbing. I'd hoped to be spared the necessity of plunging into social activities, at least for a while. While abroad I'd experienced very few such events and still preferred the comfort of my own isolation.

"I'd rather…" I began, but Grandfather cut me off.

"I knew you'd rather not go, but a little outing will do you good. You can't lock yourself up in your room with your books for ever. She is a delightful woman and has two fine daughters, Olga and Maria. You would like Olga."

"Yes, Grandfather," I said.

"And the Countess has a niece staying with her for the summer. She is also from Switzerland and you'll find her company interesting, I warrant."

"What is her name?" I asked.

I knew most of the Russians living in Switzerland, if not personally, then by name – save for the tight-knit colony of revolutionary émigrés who kept strictly to themselves.

"Rurikova. I understand her mother is in poor health and has lived in Lausanne for years."

Rurikova… No I had not met her. But the prospect of seeing someone from Switzerland, my home for so many years now, pleased me.

"Get dressed, Shota, and come downstairs in thirty minutes. Then we'll examine that intriguing specimen and decide on its value to science."

Grandfather patted me on the back and left. Meanwhile Erast was already laying out my clothes. He felt his importance now completely restored. "You see," he said almost accusingly, "Prince Platon wants you to get dressed, and how could you get dressed without my being here to dress you?"

I laughed and submitted to Erast's tyranny without further protest.

I had not seen the big dining room since my return as it was usually kept closed. Grandfather rarely used it and then only on special occasions that involved particularly honoured guests. Since my homecoming no such visitors had come. During my childhood when Grandmother still lived, its arched ceilings echoed almost daily with the laughter of guests and the clinking of glasses. Grandmother was known as one of the outstanding hostesses of her time. Czar Alexander III had been entertained in this room during his tour of Georgia. But since Grandmother's death Grandfather preferred to take his meals in a smaller dining room in another wing of the house. The fact we were to lunch in the big room today testified to the importance of the occasion, whatever it might be.

Erast escorted me to its closed doors, then, in a ceremonial gesture threw them wide open. I stopped dead in my tracks, momentarily taken aback by a sight I had not seen since early childhood.

The magnificent room spread out before me in that full Byzantine splendour so typical of Georgia's grand interiors. Tall, arched, stained glass windows depicted many of our national heroes as presented in our mythology and poetry. Queen Thamar was there in traditional dress, as was Roustavelli, St. Nino, David the Builder, and several others I could not place.

The vast dining-room table made from solid walnut stood set for three. But although the air inside the room felt as cool as that in a church or museum, the rays of sunshine splashing in through the stained glass windows gave the room a happy, even festive atmosphere.

"Here you are, Shota!" I heard Grandfather's voice behind me. "Come, I want to present my dear guest, the eminent sage and scholar, Professor Quenzano from San Sebastian."

The Basque professor stood before me, small, old and quite bald. The top of his head shone like a harvest moon, but below it a pair of bright green eyes glittered back with an unexpected youthfulness and benevolence.

"Delighted," he said in French, shaking my hand and looking at me through a thick-lensed pince-nez attached to a black ribbon.

"I wanted the Professor to see these interesting specimens of medieval stained glass," Grandfather continued. "I found them in a ruined Mingrelian castle and had them transported here by hand over the mountains. Specialists have told me they could be some of the best-preserved examples of Georgian art from the era of David the Builder in the 12th century."

Professor Quenzano inspected the stained glass sections with an intense interest. His pince-nez kept sliding down his aquiline nose, forcing him to catch it several times in mid-air.

"Of unmistakable Greek influence," he said finally, "and perhaps Byzantine. But the linear rhythms also slightly resemble the sacred pictures in the Church of Santi-Mamine in the heart of the Basque country."

I found it impossible not to like this man, both for his natural warmth and charm and also his unassuming manner – which always struck me as the genuine sign of a true scholar.

"The Professor has an interesting theory about us Georgians," Grandfather explained to me.

The Professor caught his falling pince-nez again. "Only a theory, your Excellency, but one substantiated by a good many facts."

Grandfather then signalled to the major-domo who had appeared in the door. "Supposing we lunch, Professor, and you tell us all about it?" he said.

We took our places at the enormous table and the Professor began to explain his ideas. He spoke in a low and modest voice, yet every word seemed to speak from a place of profound learning. He supported all his assertions with quotations from various scientific publications. Soon both Grandfather and I were captivated.

It appeared that the sole purpose of his coming to Tiflis had been to meet Grandfather, whose name he had received from the Academy of Sciences in St. Petersburg. The Professor then proposed his theory that the Georgians of the Caucasus and the Basques of Spain were in fact members of the same race, and this race had once ruled over most of

Europe. I found this fascinating – as the origin of the Georgians has always remained one of the great unknowns of antiquity.

It seems Professor Quenzano had been researching the equally mysterious roots of his own people and hit upon a remarkable discovery. He noticed a marked affinity between the Basque language and that of the Georgians. From this first clue he then deepened his research and soon developed a theory that the Basques and Georgians were in fact the only two remaining branches of a single great Iberian people that once inhabited most of Europe. However, due probably to some prehistoric ethnological catastrophe, the Iberian tribes had been torn asunder and largely destroyed, with only two small groups surviving. One group found refuge behind the Caucasian chain of mountains, the other in the mountains of the Basque country of Spain and France.

Grandfather listened to this exposition with rapt attention, now and then asking questions, as the food on his plate grew steadily colder.

"But how could this connection between our peoples become so completely broken, Professor?"

The Professor straightened his pince-nez and smiled. "Why do you think it is broken, your Excellency? Evidence of it is still strewn all over Europe. I have stumbled across examples in the most unexpected places. The fact is we actually bear the same name. Eastern Georgia has been called Iberia from the dawn of history. But the Spanish peninsula is also known as the Iberian peninsula. This very word is of Basque origin, not Spanish. It is composed of two Basque words, 'ibay-erri,' meaning 'the country of the river.'"

"That's true," noted Grandfather.

"And not only that, your Excellency. I have documentary evidence that before the fall of Byzantium the racial connection between our peoples was universally recognized across

Europe. Greek and Byzantine mariners who traded with both Spain and Georgia acknowledged them as the same people. Early Spanish kings addressed your kings as 'Brothers, the rulers of Iberia in the East.'"

Grandfather was clearly impressed. As long as I had known him his life followed the direction of his insatiable thirst for knowledge and new learning. The Professor's words had suddenly opened up a whole new landscape of inquiry.

"You will please stay with us, Professor? Our house is your house. Working together we might well uncover new facts with very tangible bearings on your theories."

"Undoubtedly we would," said the Professor, then added almost guiltily, "but unfortunately besides being a student, I am also a teacher, and am due back at the University for the opening of the autumn semester."

"But, Professor," Grandfather protested vigorously, "you can't waste your time dabbling in schoolbooks when great and important discoveries wait to be made."

The Professor gave a wan smile. "They will be made, your Excellency; but only if we who have been blessed with learning share our scraps of knowledge with the eager young men and women of tomorrow. It is they who will carry this knowledge into the future and in turn blaze a new trail for their children to pick up and follow."

"That's right," Grandfather agreed, "quite so."

"True science is like true love – never selfish."

To me the word 'love' sounded strange coming from the lips of a man who seemed so far removed from all such emotion.

"But surely you will stay with us until your school begins?" asked Grandfather.

"Thank you," said the Professor simply.

It was late in the afternoon when we finally rose and left the dining room. I felt elated and inspired. Close contact with men of great intellect and spirit always produces this effect on me.

Grandfather ordered his carriage be brought to the door, then he escorted the Professor upstairs to his rooms. The man was obviously fatigued by his long journey and needed to rest. He and Grandfather agreed to meet after dinner when they would go over the papers and documents the Professor had brought with him.

As we drove to the Gedeminoff estate, Grandfather remained silent, immersed in thought. He stroked his moustache, now and then emitting his familiar "Hrrumph.' Obviously he turned something over in his mind.

"Shota," he said finally, "Professor Quenzano has opened a major new field of research for me. As you know I am always hungry to discover new things. The sheer beauty of learning is in its limitlessness. The more you learn the more you realise what needs to be learnt. In this respect science possesses a kind of divine and timeless quality, just like true saintliness or true religion. God's things are eternal; only the things that operate in time are evil. But that is also why they will never be truly dangerous."

This brief contact with the small man from San Sebastian had obviously touched a latent but vital part of Grandfather's character. I could feel how this sudden re-engagement of his mind produced a sense of genuine pleasure.

Finally we arrived at Countess Gedeminoff's house to find the party in full sway. The building itself was magnificent, surrounded on all sides by an enormous English garden. The long line of landaus, barouches and cabriolets in the street, many of them bearing crests of well-known families, testified to the importance of the event. Bearded coachmen and liveried grooms stood in little groups engaged in conversation – no doubt about their respective households.

The party itself was like any other garden party. The

mistress of the house, a rather plump, pleasant lady imprisoned in fashionable summer dress, greeted each arriving guest as if he were her only and long-lost friend, then forgot about him at once. She had the appearance of a typical dowager and I found it impossible to believe she had been anything else. When I kissed her soft hand, heavy with rings, she smiled charmingly, told me she had known my father, that I was the image of him, and inquired about Paris. Oh, Paris... it was the city of her youth. How was Paris? I said that Paris was as splendid as ever, whereupon I was forgotten and left to my own devices.

Men, almost all in uniforms of some kind, and ladies in light summer dresses and wide-brimmed hats had scattered themselves over the lawns like spring flowers. Some played croquet, some gossiped and enjoyed cold punch, and some did nothing at all but tried to look interesting and high-spirited.

Boys I had known as a child, all of them now wearing dazzling military uniforms, recognized me. I found myself quickly drawn into the circles of their friends. There were many questions: Was I going to join the 17th Dragoons or go to St. Petersburg and try for the Imperial Guards? No? But surely I didn't plan to remain a civilian all my life? The diplomatic service? Well, it was my own life after all. If I wanted to waste it in the waiting rooms of Foreign Ministries, that was my business.

I was introduced to a number of young ladies, many of them charming and some beautiful. All were immediately impressed when they heard I had visited Paris just a few months earlier. To be fresh from Paris seemed to be the greatest single accomplishment a man could possess. Soon I became a centre of attraction and had to answer countless questions. Everyone appeared to have a favourite street or landmark in the City of Light, and wished to know whether it still existed. What about the Place d'Etoile? It was there. Champs Elysées? It was there. Notre Dame? There. Montmartre? There. And so on and on.

There were deviations too. An owl-like lady in a pink dress wanted to know if Poiré was really Russian, and whether his nom-de-plume of Caran d'Ache was derived from the Russian word "Karandash" or pencil.

I did not know.

A fat Major-General of the Engineering Corps wanted to know if that ugly thing, the Tour d'Eiffel, still stood where it was built eight years before, and whether it was true that its foundations were really floating in oil. He was much chagrined to learn that it appeared to stand on solid earth and swore on his word of honour that it would topple over in the first real storm.

I agreed.

A retired Gendarmerie Colonel broke through his asthma long enough to say that all Frenchmen were nihilists or republicans and should be hanged.

Eventually I was introduced to Olga and Maria Gedeminoff, the daughters of our hostess. I liked Olga. She did not ask me anything about Paris. Instead she said:

"My cousin Taya Rurikova is going to school in Paris. She is here somewhere."

The party was following its normal course and I felt a mounting desire to return to Grandfather's quiet house and listen again to Professor Quenzano.

Eventually I located Grandfather at the edge of the croquet lawn watching a game. He smiled at me then put his arm round my shoulders.

"How are you getting on, my boy?"

"Quite well thank you, sir," I said.

"Have you met many people who claimed Paris as their city of delight?"

"About fifty."

Grandfather laughed. "Never mind. Don't judge them hastily… Just wait until you know them better and besides… Oh chère Princesse," he stopped suddenly. "Allow me to present to you, my grandson, Shota d'Iberio. Shota, this is Princess Taya Rurikova, your 'compatriot' from foreign lands."

Taya Rurikova offered me her hand and smiled. Our eyes met and at this instant I fell in love for the first and last time in my life.

How can I ever describe what happened to me in that moment? It was something utterly majestic and it shook my soul to its foundations. It was like reading the Revelation of St. John by flashes of lightning; like unveiling the paintings of El Greco to the music of Bach; like dying and being born at the same moment.

Taya was tall, slender and very beautiful. But she was more than tall, slender and very beautiful. She was suddenly the only Taya in the whole world, and for me then the whole world had become only Taya.

Then a tormenting thought cut through my mind:

"I must never lose her. If I lose her, it is the end."

I do not know what I said and what she said; most probably just conventional nonsense. We could not say, or imply, or even think what we felt. I knew that she felt the same as me because I saw her face grow pale and eyes slowly turn from dark brown to jet black. No, it was not even that. I just knew.

"I must not lose her; I must not; I must not!" my mind shouted at me.

"Who has told you about me?" she said, apparently in response to something I had said.

"My grandfather and Countess Olga."

"Oh Olga! Isn't she lovely?"

"Do you ride?" I asked hastily.

"Yes," she said, "Mademoiselle Agathe and I always ride in the park."

Only then did I notice that Taya was not alone. Another woman accompanied her, older, with round black eyes and a smiling mouth. That would be Taya's governess, I thought.

"May I join you tomorrow?" I asked with a real urgency.

"Nine thirty in the morning?" she said.

"What about nine, before it gets really hot?"

"Very well," she replied. "Could you meet me at the park gate?"

Grandfather said: "You children seem to be getting on well enough. Unfortunately I must leave you now. How about if I go alone, then send Nikolai to pick you up, Shota? I have a guest at the house as you know."

Neither Taya nor I tried to detain him. Our whole lives were at stake. We could not afford to consider anything or anybody else. Not even Grandfather.

Four

TAYA'S MOTHER

I fell in love in Tiflis on a late August afternoon in 1897. But this date, as with all dates, has no meaning.

I loved Taya when the earth was without form and void, and darkness was upon the face of the deep. And I shall love her when it turns into a waterless, airless, frozen ball spinning aimlessly through black and dead endlessness.

This is neither philosophy nor poetry. I knew it the very first moment I set eyes on her face. But even if I had been blind, deaf, mute or even dead, I would have known it just as well.

I stayed at Countess Gedeminoff's party until it was impossible to stay any longer. All the time I talked to Taya. We spoke of a thousand things, because that way we could stay together. And it was simply being together that mattered, not words. Mademoiselle Agathe, Taya's governess, would not leave us alone for a second, but we did not mind. We were quite alone in our own world, and far too in love to care about secrets.

I learned several key things in the course of that afternoon. Taya's father was dead and her mother had married again, an

Austrian diplomat who had left her four years earlier, when she was taken ill. She lived in a small place in Lausanne; her condition was grave and growing steadily worse.

Taya was attending a finishing school in Paris and spent most of her free time at her mother's bedside. Her trip to the Caucasus that summer was almost accidental. Her aunt, the wealthy Countess Gedeminoff, had expressed a wish to meet Taya personally before making any provision in her will on her niece's behalf. Taya did not want to go, but her mother had begged her tearfully to do it for her sake. Taya had no strength to resist such entreaties.

For a moment terror seized me again. What would have happened had Taya's mother not prevailed? I might never have met Taya. But the next moment I knew that was impossible. I would have met Taya whatever happened; our physical meeting in Tiflis was an unimportant event compared to the profundity of the love we'd discovered. I was ashamed of the bitter fear of losing her which I experienced every few minutes since our meeting. That showed a lack of faith in our love I thought, almost a betrayal.

The next morning we rode in the park – Taya, Mademoiselle Agathe and I, with Erast as groom. Once again it was the same thing – meaningless words and the tremendous, almost delirious thrill of just being in each other's company.

Out of all the words said that morning one sentence in particular remained with me. It was something Taya said directly to me and although spoken quite casually, it carried deep significance.

"We are going back to Switzerland in about a fortnight," she said.

"At last," sighed Mademoiselle Agathe.

"Do you expect to visit Paris in the near future?" Taya asked.

"Yes," I said.

"When?"

"Very soon."

Taya made no reply but gave me a quick and penetrating glance. I could feel a profound gratitude and understanding in that look. 'He will not fail me,' she'd thought. 'He will not betray our love.' I felt her thoughts as clearly as if they had been spoken out loud.

I had not the slightest idea when I'd be able to visit Paris. I knew Grandfather expected me to stay at home for some time. But I also knew that I could not, must not be separated from Taya, even for a short period.

She read my thoughts, gave me a look that warmed me to the depths of my soul, then nodded.

"Shall we turn that way?" I said, indicating an allée to the right.

"Let's," she replied.

"This reminds me of the Bois," Mademoiselle Agathe said.

Although she may have lacked some sensitivity, even Mademoiselle Agathe felt something going on between Taya and me. What puzzled her was how we made no attempt to be alone, furthermore that our conversation remained totally free of amorous content. She could not understand we needed no outward help of any kind to know each other's feelings. We existed there together, alone and complete in our love, even within a crowd. This feeling was so powerful it seemed to possess a spiritual quality, almost as if we had been joined together as one person, and in a way that no words of love could ever hope to express.

Several times during our ride Mademoiselle Agathe fell back intentionally to give us a chance to be alone, but we always stopped and waited for her to catch up. That further bewildered her romantic French soul, and Taya and I exchanged amused glances watching her failing to understand.

I escorted Taya home and we arranged to ride again the next day.

From then on there were no more days or nights for me. My time divided simply into the periods when I was with Taya and the bleak intervals when I waited for our next meeting. We met daily, rode, walked, talked, and thrilled at the thought of meeting again the next day.

Then one morning when I rode with Erast into our stable-yard after a morning ride with Taya, one of the servants came over to say that Grandfather wanted to see me in the study. I dismounted, threw the reins to Erast and hurried up the back steps of the house.

I found Grandfather and Professor Quenzano deeply engrossed. The entire room, its tables, divans and even the floor, was covered with papers and photographs. Grandfather and the Professor were seated on the rug examining an ancient parchment. If it had not been for their venerable appearances they could easily have been mistaken for two children playing on the nursery floor. Grandfather looked up and smiled;

"Come and look at this!"

I knelt down beside him and looked at a piece of parchment.

"The Professor found it in an old Moorish house in Morocco. It was brought there from Granada by Almanzor warriors. Do you recognize it?"

The writing looked Georgian, even though the script was very ancient and I could hardly make it out.

"Is it Georgian?" I asked.

"Of course! A perfect example of the Georgian alphabet from the fourth century – a complete description of the life and work of the Apostle Andrew in Georgia... Found in

Spain! Do you understand the importance of this discovery, Shota?"

"Yes," I said.

"I have a number of those old scripts your Excellency," the Professor said indicating toward a stack of papers as yet untouched.

"Wonderful! We'll examine them in a moment. But now come here, Shota," Grandfather said standing up.

We walked to the desk and Grandfather extracted some railway tickets from the drawer. "I had planned that we should all leave for Samourzakani tomorrow morning," he said, "and already ordered the private compartment for us. But the Professor just received a telegram that cuts his visit here even shorter than expected, so I'd better stay here and work. You will go alone, Shota. The train will take you to Senaki where Vano Maradze will meet you and take you to the castle."

My heart sank. I had made arrangements to take Taya to St. David's Mountain the next morning. Words of protest were ready to leap from my lips, but Grandfather continued, a twinkle appearing in his eye:

"I drove by and saw Countess Gedeminoff this morning while you were riding," he feigned a casual air, "and I invited her, her daughters and Taya Rurikova for the trip, I knew you wouldn't mind. Unfortunately however, neither the Countess nor her daughters can go. So you'll have to be content only with Princess Rurikova's company. Her governess will also go, of course."

I saw from Grandfather's expression that he knew everything about Taya and me. Furthermore that he knew and approved. That was a wonderful moment of discovery, because Grandfather's attitude, had it been unfavourable, could have proved a serious problem for me.

Then Grandfather gave me brief instructions on what to do

after my arrival in Samourzakani; what to see and what points to take up with Maradze.

"I hope you enjoy the trip, Shota," he said.

"I'm sure I shall, sir," I said, then added breathlessly, "How can I ever thank you?"

"Thank me?" said Grandfather at first innocently. Then he gave me a direct look. "Don't thank me, Shota. Thank your Creator for whatever good things He sends your way."

Yes indeed, I had much to be thankful for... Taya and Grandfather! Never before or since have I met a man with a greater or warmer wisdom, and somehow in my mind the two became closely associated. I thought of Taya whenever I thought of Grandfather; and thinking of Taya always seemed to include Grandfather. They are the two finest people that ever entered my life.

The rest of the day was spent in preparation for the trip. Messengers ran back and forth until it was decided that I should fetch Taya and Mademoiselle Agathe in Grandfather's carriage then take them to the station.

I don't think I slept a wink that night, yet seemed to have the most beautiful dreams. I was up early only to find all my things already packed by Erast, who now rose to the occasion as never before. He was going home to his native Samourzakani and clearly felt elated. He must have spent all night polishing his dagger, because his belt's silver ornaments and his jacket's cartridge cases shone violently.

Taya, Mademoiselle Agathe, and their countless bags awaited us in the downstairs hall of the Gedeminoff's house. Mademoiselle Agathe was clearly nervous at the prospect of her first trip into 'the interior.' She expressed grave misgivings about her and Taya's safety.

"What about the mountain brigands?" she kept asking. I told her there were no such brigands, but clearly failed to convince her. The Countess received me in her private drawing room upstairs and asked me to take good care of her 'little girl.' I assured her with all my heart that I would. "I am so happy," she said, "Taya has this chance to see Georgia as it really is."

I kissed her hand and we were off.

We settled into our private coach in the train and as we left Tiflis, Mademoiselle Agathe began gradually to lose her dread of 'the interior,' and even enjoy herself. She started to express loud admiration for the passing scenery, addressing many of her long speeches directly to Erast who, although not understanding a word of French, listened with apparent great interest.

Erast proved invaluable. He'd packed sufficient provisions for a month's voyage and every one of our meals turned into a veritable feast. Somehow he coaxed Mademoiselle Agathe into taking a few drinks of Kakhetian wine, which set her off giggling. This turned into a blessing because she at last stopped asking her endless questions. As for Taya, she scored an immediate triumph over Erast, and he collected fresh field flowers for her at every stop, which everybody found touching.

Taya herself was no less wide-eyed in her excitement. Her passionate love for nature seemed to grow at every turn and she repeatedly praised the magnificent scenery sliding past the windows. She wanted to know everything about the country and listened avidly to my inadequate explanations.

"This is more beautiful than Switzerland…" she kept repeating, looking at the snow-capped Greater Caucasus mountains to the north, now sharply outlined against the blue sky and stretching across the horizon. "… and much, much wilder. Tell me about it, please!"

I told her all I knew. As the largest and highest mountain chain in Europe the Caucasus stretched in an unbroken barrier from the Black Sea to the Caspian Sea, a distance of over

700 miles. From time immemorial it had acted like a gigantic comb through which numerous waves of migrants and conquerors had passed – some of whom ended up making it their home.

Our train passed through the many ancient towns of central Georgia then entered the beautiful province of Mingrelia (or Samegrelo). Darkness approached when we finally arrived at the small railway station nearest our estate. The countryside around it exuded a wild beauty, with grey granite mountains and blue-green pine forests crowding in on all sides. From here we would take a mountain road to Zugdidi, ferry across the Ingur river and only then reach the principality of Samourzakani.

Vano Maradze, a slight man of perhaps fifty-five and dressed in a brown suit, waited for us on the platform. Around him stood his group of men from Samourzakani, all dressed in the full splendour of mountain warriors. They wore fur hats, tight-fitting boots, long coats, breast cartridge-cases and daggers in scabbards attached to their belts. A truly handsome and colourful body of men; but for those unfamiliar with the dress of the region's peace-loving peasantry – quite awe-inspiring. I noticed poor Mademoiselle Agathe begin to turn white. So this was the terrible 'interior,' and those the 'mountain brigands' she had heard so much about in Paris before starting her Caucasian voyage.

The moment our train came to a stop, Vano Maradze barked out commands and the men swarmed into the carriage to begin taking down our luggage. When one of these mountain warriors approached the poor governess and attempted to take the bag she carried, she dropped it to the floor with a terrified shriek. The man, tall and handsome with a black moustache, reacted by showing her all his teeth in an embarrassed smile, no doubt equally shocked by such a strange reaction from this pretty foreign woman.

"Welcome, Master," Vano Maradze greeted me. He had an intelligent face and spoke good Russian without any trace of an accent. I offered him my hand, which he shook respectfully. "This is most unfortunate..." he mumbled. "Most unfortunate indeed..."

"What is unfortunate?" I asked.

Maradze explained that due to recent torrential rain, the roads had been washed out in some sections and the only possible way to reach Samourzakani would now be on horseback. He was deeply apologetic. Prince Platon had not told him there would be ladies in the party – which if he had known he would have advised the trip be postponed for a few days.

"How long will it take to reach Samourzakani?" I asked.

"At least six or seven hours' hard riding," answered Maradze. "Therefore I suggest that we stop at the castle of Prince Dadiani for the night. It's just a few kilometres from here and he will be happy to host you and the ladies as his guests. In the meantime I'll see if I can get a carriage over here from Samourzakani."

Taya was brought in on the conference and clapped her hands in delight when she discovered our predicament. "Wonderful! We'll ride tonight. Mademoiselle Agathe and I are excellent riders. Six or seven hours in the saddle would be a great experience. Let's start at once, please!"

Mademoiselle Agathe, however, showed less enthusiasm at the idea. She urged us to spend the night at the Dadiani castle. But Taya would not listen so we decided to start out for Samourzakani as soon as we changed into our riding clothes.

Soon our luggage was packed onto the spare horses which Maradze had brought from the estate and we started out through a narrow mountain gorge. It was a colourful cavalcade. Some of Maradze's men rode at the head while others formed a sort of rearguard. They pulled out their rifles and rode with them set across their saddles, traditional style. Although the precaution was needless in a region now peaceful for many decades, tradition is very dear to the Georgian heart. Men should never be denied the privilege, albeit harmless, of showing off their readiness to fight.

As darkness gathered, the outriders lit oil-soaked torches and galloped up and down the mountain trail in displays of reckless horsemanship. The presence of Taya and Mademoiselle Agathe fanned their gallantry. In trying to outdo each other in feats of increasing daring, one enthusiast finally fired off his rifle. The loud report echoed through the mountains and Mademoiselle Agathe nearly fell from her horse. Maradze quickly reproached the culprit and the fireworks stopped.

But who could deny the intensely romantic atmosphere surrounding our journey. I could see Taya was thrilled.

"What a beautiful country and what fine people," she said with great feeling. "And their ways haven't changed for centuries."

"A German traveller once called this 'The Land of the Last Knights'," I told her.

"How fitting. I can feel that spirit of the Middle Ages filling the air, Shota. I'm falling in love with your country!"

That was the first time she had ever called me 'Shota' and it touched me deeply. As we were riding side by side, I took her hand and kissed it silently.

Then the moon rose up above us; a wonderful round and yellow Mingrelian moon. Its silver light quickly transformed the countryside into a fairy tale of jagged cliffs and shimmering mountain brooks. Then somewhere over our heads an owl began to hoot.

About halfway to the estate we halted beside a mountain stream. The men unsaddled the horses and turned them out to graze. Campfires soon began to crackle. Wine and bread were produced from the saddle packs, and then the tantalizing smell of roasting lamb filled the air. Somebody unpacked an ancient stringed instrument called a chonguri and soon its melody began to float out into the cool night air. Before long somebody started to sing a Georgian ballad – the words following the usual themes of love, war and sorrow. Within minutes even Mademoiselle Agathe was carried away by the spirit of the occasion.

"What a night for romance," she sighed, casting her eyes towards the young man who had frightened her at the station.

While Erast brewed us tea over the camp fire, Taya and I walked in silence down by the stream. Although Taya clearly felt fatigued by the ride, the nervous excitement of our adventure kept her senses wide awake.

To the plaintive sounds of the chonguri drifting over from the camp, a masculine voice sang out the words:

"On your little finger I'd rest
If I were a thimble of gold.
Your tender feet I'd caress
If I were a weed by the road."

"On a night like this one feels that dying could be so easy," Taya said. "Surely nothing can surpass this night in its beauty. So why then live on through all the ugliness that might follow?"

"Everything has a purpose," I said, "even ugliness."

"Even suffering?" There was a sudden sadness in her voice.

"Even suffering," I answered. "But why speak of things like that, Taya?"

This was the first time too, I had called her Taya. The sound of her name touched something deep inside me.

"I'm thinking of Mother," she said, now in a different, tragic voice. Two tears sparkled in the moonlight and rolled down her cheeks. Suddenly I felt an overpowering urge to take her in my arms and kiss away those tears. But instead I only said:

"I understand that she is ill."

"She is dying slowly," Taya said miserably, "and it seems so unjust. She is not old and she loves life more than anyone I know, Shota..." her voice broke momentarily.

"What is it, Taya my dearest?"

"I hope so much you'll meet my mother soon. Not many people are kind to those who are about to die," she said simply. "They want to hurry away and forget. Death upsets people, which isn't right; it's unnatural. But you are different, Shota. You couldn't be otherwise."

The words of the singer blended with the bubbling water of the stream:

"If I were your secret thought
I'd always live in your heart.
If I were your shadow, my love,
Then we never would part..."

"She is all I have... all I had, in the world," Taya continued now full of emotion. "She was always so good to me, even when the whole world tore at her like a pack of wolves. When she married Otto von Lemberg the family turned away from her. He was a cruel man, but she never let him hurt me in any way. She has stood by me through so many bad and sad times. I'd rather die a thousand times over than hurt her in any way, Shota... or let anyone hurt her, especially now that she has so little time to live."

She stopped, slipped her hand quickly into the neck of her blouse and lifted out a small object on a gold chain.

"Look, Shota," she said.

In the moonlight I could just make out a round gold medallion bearing a tiny image of the Madonna.

"Mother gave it to me in Paris when she first fell ill and had to go to Lausanne. She said this would keep me, protect me from evil and guide me toward health and happiness." She lifted the icon to her lips and kissed it reverently. We resumed our walk in silence and soon approached an open space where stepping stones had been placed across the stream. They lay there like black blocks in the foaming white water and I realised we'd stumbled across a mountain trail used by shepherds in the search for fresh grass for their sheep. Beside the trail stood a wooden shrine in the shape of a cross containing a small image of the Virgin under a gable-roof. In the recess below the icon, several coins glittered in the moonlight.

We stopped to look.

"What does it say there?" Taya asked, pointing to a line of Georgian script written under the icon.

I strained my eyes and read: "If you have, give; if you need, take."

"What does it mean?" Taya asked.

"Just what it says Taya. The poorer travellers take a few coins if they need them and the richer travellers put some in. You'll find shrines like this all over these mountains."

I took some silver coins from my pocket and placed them on the plank, not noticing Taya take off her medallion and chain. Then suddenly I saw her place them among the coins.

"Taya...!" I said, but she stopped me.

"I know Mother would wish me to do this, Shota... Perhaps it will bring luck and happiness to someone else. I have so much that even if I keep giving it away day and night until the end of time, I'll never spend all my happiness."

She shivered as if growing chilly. A thin fog rose over the river and she took my hand firmly.

"Let's go back," she said quietly. Suddenly there was no more sadness in her voice.

Five

FATHER SHALVA

THE slightest hint of a summer dawn had already appeared in the eastern sky when we reached the rain-swollen Ingur river and had ourselves ferried across. Now we were in Samourzakani and my heart beat a little faster. This was the land of my forefathers, and every rock on the trail suddenly seemed friendly and personal to me.

I had not seen Samourzakani for many years, but found myself again impressed by the loveliness of the countryside. The rolling hills were covered with orderly rows of vines – more than I remembered from before. The lowland fields too were all cultivated and cut across with irrigation ditches. Now every bit of arable earth seemed to have been broken and worked. Samourzakani was blossoming like a gigantic flower, green, fresh and clean.

"Wasn't this area deserted before?" I asked Maradze who rode beside Taya and me.

"Yes," he answered cagily, choosing his words with care, "it was… before Prince Platon gave it away to the peasants."

"It's good to see," I said.

"To see, yes; but not to manage," Maradze sighed. "I am

having much trouble. People are growing restless. They forget they hold these lands only temporarily. They are acting like lords and masters; losing respect for their betters."

Poor Maradze may have had his problems but he failed to notice the larger picture inside which they were all set. I felt genuinely sorry for him but could offer no solace.

"The world is falling to pieces," he continued. "I can see the handwriting on the wall all around... Big estates are disintegrating... The Marchanis had to sell their lands across the river to some people from the north who want to build a resort then rent cottages to tourists. The princely estates are choking in debt while their masters are dancing in St. Petersburg and Paris. The end of the world is upon us."

"Or perhaps the beginning of a new one?" Taya ventured quietly.

There was a veiled irony in Maradze's voice as he answered. "I wish I could think so, Princess. It is not merely my own opinion. I have spoken to wise men who have been here a long time. They all agree things are going from bad to worse. They have never seen it like this before."

"Everything changes," Taya said with an unusual note of seriousness in her voice. "Once I heard a story about butterflies that live only one day. They are born in the early morning when the sun is young and bright, and by noon they reach middle age. By then they are no longer the carefree butterflies they had been before. But at noon a new generation of butterflies is suddenly born and starts fluttering in the sun. When the sun begins to set the old generation start to worry... 'The world is coming to an end' they say to the young butterflies. 'Look! The sun is growing colder, dark shadows settle in the valleys. Things were never this way when we were your age. They were brighter and better. This is the end, children. We are old and wise and we know everything.' Then they die, convinced that everything is finished. But the sun rises again the next morning and new butterflies flutter over the flowers as bright and carefree as ever."

Maradze made no answer to this and we rode on in silence.

Shortly afterwards we turned into a wide valley and there, straight ahead, atop a small knoll I suddenly saw Samourzakani castle silhouetted against a pale green sky, sombre and imposing. Built of dark Mingrelian stone many centuries ago, it had nobly withstood the assault of time, its grey walls and tall watchtowers rising starkly out of a sheer cliff. Our horses, sensing the food and rest ahead, neighed and pranced, clattering their hooves eagerly against the broken stone of the road – also looking forward to their homecoming.

"This is just like a page from a fairytale," Taya said. "It's so unreal, so beautiful."

"Magnifique," echoed Mademoiselle Agathe.

"It's sad to think that all this is going to perish," sighed Maradze.

At this moment a guard's voice from the nearest watchtower shouted out:

"Four o'clock of a clear morning and all is well."

Another guard repeated this cry from another tower, then another, and still another. Samourzakani was welcoming us with the announcement of a new day and the assurance of peace and contentment on earth.

"Four o'clock of a clear morning and all is well!"

A heavy drawbridge clattered down with mournful creaks and we rode across the moat to a gate made of enormous cedar planks reinforced with iron bolts. It swung open slowly, admitting us into the castle's spacious courtyard.

A feeling of security and wellbeing enveloped me, along with, I confess, the tempting thought of a soft bed.

The next morning I rose late and spent the better part of

the day with Maradze going through his books – which inter-
ested me not at all – and looking over the various portions of
the estate which he insisted on showing me. Meanwhile Taya
and Mademoiselle Agathe continued to rest, clearly exhausted by the trip. Although missing their company, I dutifully
studied Maradze's accounts. Once or twice he tried to point
out, very gently, the consequences of my grandfather's generous follies. But I never encouraged him and he soon understood his complaints fell on deaf ears. His stance was made
doubly difficult by the fact that the estate now genuinely
flourished in spite of Grandfather's generosity. He could not
understand why or how, but had to admit that was all going
remarkably well.

The dinner was simple but beautifully served. Taya and
Mademoiselle Agathe came down and I insisted that Maradze
also dine with us. Before long we were all merrily eating and
drinking as Maradze told us stories about Samourzakani and
its former landlords. He displayed remarkable skills as a his-
torian and regaled us with many amusing anecdotes about my
family and their predecessors.

After dinner we played dominoes and listened to Taya
playing the piano, which she did charmingly, particularly
when accompanied by Mademoiselle Agathe's fine soprano
voice. We retired early. The pleasant, carefree routine of the
castle had started to take its hold, and it felt good.

I always think there is something about life in the countryside that makes one calmer and more content. This is especially true of the Georgian countryside, which more than any
other, seems to have retained that mellow flavour and slower
pace of the centuries before ours. Time glided by in a leisure-
ly way to create a happy and cloudless period for Taya and
me and our steadily growing love. Even Mademoiselle
Agathe developed a taste for the bucolic life and often took to
following Maradze about the estate, listening to his tales told

in broken French – and of course asking him repeated questions. I noticed too that Maradze started to use increasing amounts of wax on his moustache – a sure sign that romance might be afoot.

On the first Sunday after our arrival, the inhabitants of the neighbouring villages arranged a fête and tournament in our honour. These knightly jousting sessions or 'jiritoba' had been an integral part of Georgian life for centuries. During the days leading up to the event the castle and nearby villages began to buzz like swarms of excited of bees. Young men polished their weapons and riding equipment. They then groomed their horses and held practice jousting sessions outside their villages. Girls started trying on their better clothes and even the older men and women joined in the increasingly festive atmosphere. Then one day the castle servants suddenly began spreading sawdust over the courtyard where the jiritoba would take place. They pitched tents for guests and spectators and started to prepare for an enormous open-air feast. As was the tradition, only the best food and wine would be served, and to every person that attended regardless of rank or status. On the morning of the fête, pots suddenly started to boil, barbecue pits smoke and the air fill with the most delicious aromas.

After morning Mass the guests started to arrive in droves – on horseback, in carriages, in open carts and on foot. Soon the big courtyard began to fill with men and women dressed in festival attire. Grey-bearded elders proudly displayed their best family daggers and swords. They formed a special group under the canopy reserved for the lords of the castle – in this case Taya and myself – and were to act as judges, with myself as final authority. By noon the village jiritoba teams, each flying its own banner, started arriving on prancing horses, the teams being careful not to mix with each other. As they rode into the courtyard the crowd greeted them enthusiastically, to complete a magnificent spectacle. The men, handsome and fit, wore their finest traditional dress, each one looking a perfect portrait of manhood. The cream of the local youth had transformed themselves, head to toe, into young knights. Now they arrived at the castle for their day's jousting.

For the first time since my arrival back in Georgia I had to don the traditional costume of my people, complete with the ancient 'Sword of the d'Iberios.' The costume had been prepared by Maradze, and although at first I found the thought of wearing it embarrassing, the moment I put it on I felt I'd worn it all my life. Taya's eyes stretched wide when she saw me, and Mademoiselle Agathe gasped.

Finally Taya and I took our places under the purple canopy. The moment was greeted by a loud chorus of welcomes. Then the elders were introduced to me one by one by Maradze – who also wore a magnificent traditional costume. The tournament began with horsemen racing past our stand like individual hurricanes, each man trying to outdo the others in, it seemed, reckless abandon. Swords sparkled and flashed over heads like bolts of lightning as the riders came charging straight toward us at full gallop. Only when it seemed inevitable they would crash into our group, did they finally swerve aside and ride triumphantly away.

Then the jiritoba tournament began in earnest. It seemed as if the full colour and pomp of medieval Georgia had suddenly resurrected itself into the present. We witnessed mock fights and races between individual horsemen; entire troops of men assaulting each other; swords ringing out and hooves clattering. How they managed to avoid wounding each other amidst all the violence and chaos remained a complete mystery. Riding at full gallop and gripping long wooden lances, the horsemen then tried to unseat each other. Under the fearful impact some unfortunates literally flew up into the air, but miraculously always managed to find their feet and walk away undamaged – save perhaps for some wounded pride. They were then allowed to remount and try to find redemption in the next event. The sole reward for winners came as acclamation from the crowd, and especially Taya, who applauded spiritedly at every feat of daring. For this the men seemed almost ready to break their necks, even kill themselves.

Gradually individual contestants began to emerge as jiritoba heroes – selected from the consistent winners and those who stood out in the events. One was the young man who frightened Mademoiselle Agathe when he grabbed her bag at the station. Now the thrilled governess recognized him as an old acquaintance and smiled every time he passed our stand. The young man reciprocated with burning glances. Clearly conscious of being watched by this one lady he strove yet more gallantly to prove himself worthy of her attention.

"Who is he?" Taya asked Maradze.

"His name is Tarash Rama; he comes from a mountain village," Maradze explained, clearly a little concerned at Mademoiselle Agathe's behaviour.

"He's a wonderful rider," Taya said.

"Yes," Maradze admitted reluctantly, "one of the finest to have ridden a horse."

But the highlight of the day for me was the performance of Erast, who gave a quite superb account of himself for our castle team. Once in the saddle he seemed an entirely different man – graceful, swift, reckless and cunning; hard to believe this was the same slow and stubborn Erast who plagued me with his staunch faithfulness. Taya rewarded him with her special attention, which left him brimming with pride.

Soon the team contests finished, with the mountain village of Tarash Rania proclaimed the winner by the elders. Our own castle team finished second, much to the chagrin of Erast.

Next came the displays of individual horsemanship. Here

young riders launched into death-defying feats, encouraged by passionate cries from the crowd. They charged like madmen, whirling themselves about in their saddles like dervishes, throwing lances high into the air and catching them, firing rifles, swinging their swords with unruly abandon. Some young women in the crowd started throwing their handkerchiefs on the ground. The men, galloping at breakneck speeds, then scooped them up in their hands as if the small scraps of linen were in fact items of treasure. Taya also dropped her handkerchief and caused such a mad scramble I felt sure it would result in casualties. Fortunately there were none, and in the end it was our own Erast who emerged holding it triumphantly above his head. He dismounted, walked over to Taya, returned the handkerchief, then according to tradition knelt down and reverently kissed the hem of her dress. A touching scene, and I saw tears in Taya's eyes as she returned the handkerchief to Erast as a reward for gallantry.

This greatly impressed Mademoiselle Agathe who immediately threw her own handkerchief straight into the path of Tarash Rania, who retrieved it without any trouble or competition. Then to her great disappointment, instead of returning it to her, he kissed it, stuck it in his silver belt and rode swiftly away. Somewhat sourly Maradze explained that she had committed a serious faux-pas by throwing her handkerchief to an individual rider. Now Tarash was justified in considering this a sign of her special favour. Mademoiselle Agathe appeared slightly abashed but laughed it off.

The tournament then finished and the feast began – a tremendous Georgian banquet with the usual abundance of food, floods of wine and much toasting. These ceremonial feasts are deeply rooted within the tradition of our people and date back into the mists of time. Even today no other social event can rival them in lavishness or exuberance.

When darkness fell over the castle the feast continued by

the light of huge bonfires burning in the courtyard. Silver cups clinked; fresh barrels of wine were constantly rolled up from the cellar and whole lambs barbecued on turning spits. Dripping fat hissed on the coals and clouds of white smoke rose above the pits. Amazingly, in spite of the enormous amount of wine consumed, we saw no arguments, harsh words or unruly acts of drunkenness. In Georgia to become sloppily drunk is considered a disgrace. Certainly voices and laughter grew louder; the clinking of glasses more enthusiastic, but still the voices, laughter and clinking remained friendly and good natured.

After a while Taya, Maradze and I retreated to the drawing room. As we sipped coffee and commented on the day's events our attention was suddenly drawn by an excited clamour of voices down in the courtyard. I sent Erast to investigate. He came back a few minutes later smiling ear to ear.

"What happened?" I asked.

"Nothing much, Master," he answered, the grin still wide across his face. "A woman was abducted and taken away to the hills."

I relaxed. This was a charming and ancient custom among the enamoured youth of our villages. A man would 'abduct' his sweetheart in a seemingly violent but actually prearranged way, riding her off as her male relatives usually gave a spirited but futile 'chase.' The whole event would end up in a marriage ceremony and yet another tremendous feast with everyone involved in the drama taking part.

I explained the practice to an amused Taya. We drank more coffee, then I noticed Maradze not enjoying it as much as he might.

"Erast," I turned to our Sancho Panza, "go and ask the French lady to join us. She is somewhere outside watching the feast."

There was a long pause before Erast answered. "No, Master," he said, "she is not outside."

"No? What do you mean?"

Erast grinned. "It is the French lady who has been abducted."

"What!" cried Maradze leaping to his feet.

"Yes," Erast explained, still grinning. "Tarash Rania took her on his horse and rode away into the hills."

Although a potentially dire situation, I couldn't prevent a smile from touching my lips. Taya on the other hand, unable to understand Erast's words, almost fainted when we explained how poor Mademoiselle Agathe had fallen innocent victim to this local custom.

"Heavens!" she cried. "What will they do to her?"

"Nothing, Taya," I tried to placate her. "No one would ever mistreat a woman in this place... Not as much as a kiss without her consent. She is probably having the thrill of her life."

But Maradze took a more serious view. "I'd better go and straighten it out," he declared resolutely.

He ordered Erast to bring his horse and select a few riders.

"I am going too!" Taya insisted. "Poor Mademoiselle is probably dying of fright by now. And she doesn't understand one word of Russian or Georgian!"

"How far is it to the village?" I asked.

"About two hours ride but the roads are bad," Maradze said.

"I'm coming!" Taya repeated.

Maradze and I protested but to no avail. Taya would not stay at home and wait. She felt it her personal duty to rescue her governess.

"Get a horse for the Princess," Maradze finally ordered. We left the castle unnoticed by the merrymakers and rode hard over the winding mountain trails up to a small village tucked away under the cliffs. We found Mademoiselle Agathe terrified but unharmed. Tarash Rania had taken her straight to his old mother who now stroked Mademoiselle's hair trying to console her with tender Georgian words – which of course were pure Greek to the poor governess. Although by now almost hysterical, somewhere in the hysteria one detected a tiny hint of pride. To be abducted by a handsome mountain warrior... was this not also a memorable adventure for the town-bred young woman of Passy?

On our arrival Mademoiselle Agathe promptly fainted straight into Maradze's arms. I then explained to Tarash and his bewildered mother how the whole thing had been a tragic mistake.

"I thought so," the old woman shook her head ruefully. "She was crying too much even for a happy bride."

We started our way back to the castle led by one of the castle servants carrying a flaming torch, then came Maradze with Mademoiselle Agathe in his arms – she had wisely chosen to remain in a swoon; followed by Taya, Erast and me. Another torch-bearer brought up the rear. We were in no particular hurry and rode at varying speeds until gradually our cavalcade stretched over perhaps a quarter of a mile. Soon the torch of our advance guard could hardly be seen as Taya and I talked and laughed about Mademoiselle Agathe's great adventure as well as her obvious infatuation with Maradze. Gradually we fell even farther behind.

As we approached our valley the trail narrowed into a track cut into a sheer cliff high above a swirling mountain river. As we made our way beside the vertical granite wall, suddenly we heard a dull roar directly ahead. Then the lights of the advance guard abruptly vanished. We reined in our horses and waited in the darkness – to hear only a roaring silence. We summoned our torch-bearer then advanced cautiously forward until we came to a large pile of fresh earth and boulders lying across the trail. It seemed one of the frequent mountain slides had come down to completely block our path.

We were trapped.

Perched on that ledge in a tight group we discussed our options. Erast dismounted and attempted to climb the heap, but it proved too large and dangerously unstable. Several large boulders promptly gave way to roll over the edge of the precipice. I ordered him back.

Then I heard a faint voice and recognised it as Maradze on the other side of the slide trying to make himself heard. He had a strong voice but I could barely make out his words:

"Are... you... safe?"

"We are safe!" I shouted back, but my voice never carried. Erast took over. He cupped his hands around his mouth and repeated my message so piercingly it nearly deafened us.

"Stay there!" came Maradze's reply, "and don't touch the rocks. I will send men from the castle to clear the trail. Meanwhile go to the Monastery of Iliori and wait there."

"Very well," I said and Erast re-transmitted my message using the full power of his leather-bag lungs.

We held a quick conference. Erast told me the Monastery of Iliori was a small, half-abandoned monastery some two or three miles from our trail. A few monks still lived among the ruins, leading hermit-like existences. But, as it was by far the nearest place with any food and shelter, we decided to go. Erast now assumed leadership of our group and we rode on in silence.

It took almost an hour to negotiate the overgrown goat trails, then finally we spotted the monastery – a cluster of dark buildings encircled by a partly demolished stone wall. Its small iron gate had been securely bolted and I rattled it vigorously to attract attention.

Eventually a flickering light appeared within the enclosure and a tall young man wearing a monk's robe, lantern in his hand, appeared behind the gate. He lifted his lantern to light up our faces.

I explained that we were from Samourzakani castle and needed temporary shelter.

"Women are not allowed inside the gate," said the young monk looking at Taya. "Please wait here. I will speak to Father Shalva."

He disappeared and returned shortly with Father Shalva. He stood behind the gate tall, ascetic and very ancient, his thin white beard waving slightly in the breeze. Once again I repeated my story. The old hermit remained silent for a few moments leaning on his staff, stroking his beard. Then a smile creased the edges of his lips and his severe face suddenly transformed into one of kindness.

"Open the gate my son," he said to the young monk. "The house of God is available to all who need its shelter."

The bolt creaked and we walked on inside. Father Shalva led Taya and myself to a small building which must have been the monastery's former refectory. Meanwhile the young monk looked after Erast and our torch-bearer. Father Shalva placed his lantern on the heavy oak table and as he did so a number of superb mosaics were suddenly revealed spread across the walls and vaulted ceiling. Many were cracked and broken, but the overall effect was of a once magnificent room.

"What wonderful work," I said quietly. "Who did it?"

Father Shalva stroked his beard and looked at the mosaics dispassionately. "They were made by Syrian fathers in the fifth century, then restored by Queen Thamar during her visit to Samourzakani."

I translated the Father's words to Taya. As soon as he understood she spoke no Georgian he continued in perfect Russian.

"The Queen first came here to witness the marriage of the Byzantine Princess Anna to Prince George d'Iberio. She liked this place and visited it several times during her reign."

The young monk brought in an earthen jug of goat's milk and several flat breads. Although we were not hungry the cold milk tasted good.

"We are sorry to cause you all this trouble, Father," I said. "We understand that you have broken a rule for us..."

"Yes I have," answered Father Shalva simply. Then his smile returned, "but it was man's rule not God's." He gave Taya a long, searching look as if studying her face minutely. "Is your name Taya my daughter?"

"Yes Father." Taya said.

"Taya... Taya... A rare and beautiful name. Then I think I have something for you Taya."

He held up the small gold icon which Taya had deposited at the shrine by the river crossing and looked at its reverse side.

"The inscription reads 'To Taya from Mother'. A pious man brought it to me. You should keep it for your mother's sake. It is a token of her great faith and it is meant to be yours."

Father Shalva spoke with such clarity and simplicity it seemed to leave Taya speechless. Silently she took the medallion and slipped it back around her neck. Then the Father stood up and leant on his staff.

"Would you children care to come out and enjoy the night?" he asked softly. "Unfortunately we have no accommodation here for ladies, but God in his wisdom has provided all mankind with the glory of His heavens. Tonight the air is warm and a moon is coming out over the mountain."

We thanked him and stepped outside into a night that was indeed enchanting. Somewhere not far away came the sound of a brook bubbling through the monastery grounds, and above it a lonely nightingale sang, adding its spell to the sleeping world.

"Here," said Father Shalva, as we approached a large flat

stone near the brook. "Sit down. We are not in the grounds here so no one can reproach us for breaking any rules." He sat down and we followed his example. "Queen Thamar liked to sit here alone and at night to contemplate her love; a love that was so great she felt it could never die."

Taya and I waited in silence for Father Shalva to continue. I can honestly say that in that moment we never felt closer to each other, nor more in love. The presence of this saintly man had the effect of elevating and binding our intimacy; drawing us so close we seemed almost to be one person.

"Don't be afraid of your love," Father Shalva said after a short pause. "Love, like everything else made by God, is pure and deathless. Death exists only in the thought of man, and everything he touches turns to death only because he insists on measuring everything with his own mortal measurement. But there are times when God's power breaks through such measurement. That is when time falls away and the doors of eternity swing open, as happened to Queen Thamar and the man she loved."

He paused briefly.

"They could not have their love, the great Queen and the humble poet, and there came a time when they knew they had no alternative but to part for ever. Pain and despair filled both their hearts. Then one night as Roustavelli sat at his Queen's feet meditating on their unhappy predicament, God gave Thamar wisdom which even she had never known before and she spoke His words. 'What is our love, Roustavelli, if we are so afraid to lose it? If it is indeed as great as we think, how then can it ever die? Have no fear, my beloved. If it lives for ever then we shall never lose it. If it disappears, it has not been worth our despair. Go away and love me even as I love you and be heartened, for there is no death to anything touched by God.' As she spoke the darkness in their hearts suddenly lifted. When they parted, men thought they had lost their love irredeemably, but they knew otherwise. They knew they had lost something, only to have it for ever."

From somewhere in the distance we could just hear the sound of a human voice starting to sing. It seemed our torch-bearer had joined in with the nightingale.

"Hosts of men have been born since that day," Father Shalva continued. "Hosts of men have enjoyed what they thought was love, and hosts of men have also thought that it had died. But Thamar's and Roustavelli's love lives on today, enshrined in the hearts of their people. It continues in huts and palaces, in mountains and valleys, in songs and prayers, in hopes and despairs, endless, measureless, timeless."

Father Shalva fell silent. Neither Taya nor I had any words to add. The only sound to reach us was now the torch-bearer's song. Although I could distinguish no words I recognized the melody as a folk ballad composed to the verses of the same great poet.

Father Shalva rose and leaned heavily on his staff. We stood too. Without saying a word we bowed our heads and the old man blessed us silently. "The rock slide is all but cleared," he said simply. "If you wish you may proceed on your way. May God give you His wisdom to live and love for ever, all the way into His great deathlessness."

We rode back in silence. Even Erast and the torch-bearer seemed to sense our mood and never disturbed us with any words. We arrived at the slide to find the large boulders already removed and we were able to pass through the dangerous section with the workmen holding up torches to light the way.

Soon the walls and watchtowers of the castle appeared. They seemed strangely silent even though the lights in the inhabited quarters still burned brightly. As we approached the moat, I heard the familiar cry of the first guard:

"Three o'clock of a clear morning…"

I waited for the usual ending of the call '...and all is well' but it never came. I reined in my horse so abruptly that the animal reared.

"Taya! Taya! Something is wrong."

"Why?" she asked, alarmed.

"Because... listen!"

"Three o'clock of a clear morning..." came the call from another tower.

Taya had grown familiar with the guards' cries during her stay in the castle. "Yes, Shota. All is not well!"

Swiftly we galloped across the drawbridge and in through the gates to be greeted by a totally unexpected sight. The courtyard was still filled with people, but a quite different crowd from the one we had left behind – one now utterly sober, silent and motionless.

We halted our horses and I saw Maradze approach. I could not see his face but his steps were heavy. He stopped and spoke haltingly, with great effort.

"A messenger... has just come from the station. Prince Didi Platon... has left us..."

He could not continue because tears choked him up completely. Suddenly I felt the weight of the entire world fall on my heart. I could not speak, cry, or even think. And then I felt Taya's hand on mine. And I heard her voice, as a bare whisper:

"There is no death to those touched by God, Shota. They go away from the mortal world – to live for ever."

Six

FRANÇOIS

THE Marseilles-Paris Express burrowed its way through the low-hanging fog of a cold and dismal February morning. We had passed Melun, the last large town before Paris, and now neared our destination – the Gare de Lyon. Through the occasional hole in the fog I could see rows of naked, rain-soaked lindens and willows. Patches of black earth rushed past my window and disappeared into the mist as our engine disgorged clouds of grey smoke. La Belle France did not look so belle that morning. The face of Erast sitting on the opposite bench in my compartment wore a mournful expression. He clearly felt quite out of his element in this strange country – a tall lean man wearing his first European suit complete with celluloid collar and black tie. The outfit left him painfully self-conscious. He sat erect and quiet, the very picture of intense melancholy, blinking at the rivulets of rainwater running down the window glass. His thoughts were far away, back in sun-drenched Samourzakani. Clearly he could not understand for the life of him what force could tear me away from the green land of my birth and fling me into this unfriendly, cold and misty country.

Five months had passed since that tragic night at the castle when the watchtower guards brought me news of Grandfather's death. These months had been very difficult for me. I was confronted by a great number of strange and complex formalities, all needing attention, yet all seemed so incongruous when set against the background of such incomprehensible sorrow.

Grandfather left this world as simply and directly as he had done everything in his life. Professor Quenzano found him in his easy chair in the study, an open book in his hands, an expression of serenity on his face. Apparently God had summoned him with startling suddenness but Grandfather had still been ready to answer His call. He stepped out of his physical frame as one would step out of a carriage at the end of a long trip. He had enjoyed the journey and now appreciated the prospect of rest, a true Christian homecoming after completing his earthly tasks.

Grandfather's body was taken to Samourzakani for burial and the entire population of the province came out to bid their last farewell to the most loved man they had known. Every man in the crowd wore a black slip over his dagger and cartridge cases. Every woman showed herself deep in mourning. Only then did I realize the extent to which Grandfather's life had not been in vain; and how to all those grief-stricken, silent people, he had never died.

A delegation from Khevsuretia, a remote mountain province in Georgia, especially impressed me. Blue-eyed, handsome, taciturn giants wearing the traditional costume of their crusading forefathers; coats of mail with the cross on chest and back, low-visored iron helmets in their hands. They entered the church in a silent group, stood for a few long minutes before the bier, then placed a long, straight crusader sword with a cross-shaped handle on the casket and left without uttering a word. I never heard their names, nor learned their history, nor what connection they had ever had with Grandfather. They looked and acted like ghosts from the past who had lost their way, to find themselves momentarily propelled up here among the living.

Two people throughout this trying time gave me comfort and the courage to face what remained of my life. One was Taya, the wonderful Taya who conducted herself with such tact and understanding that she never seemed in my way, yet I never felt alone for a moment. Another was Erast. He had shown himself not only a perfect servant but also a devoted friend. Somehow I felt he was that part of Grandfather's life still left inside me. No longer did he irritate or bother me. Instead I had grown to depend on his ever faithful presence. I found it a real comfort when he said, as we returned to the castle after the funeral:

"I shall always remain with you Prince Shota... wherever you go."

"I may go away and never come back, Erast," I said.

"I shall go with you."

"But you have your own life to live," I protested half-heartedly. "Don't you want to marry and settle down in Samourzakani? I will help you as much as I can."

"No," he said. "I promised Prince Didi Platon to take care of you. I shall honour my promise unto death."

I embraced him and from that point on, Erast became an integral part of my life.

Taya left Tiflis shortly thereafter to return to school. Our parting was sad but not tragic. It had been decided between us that as soon as I put my affairs in order, I would come to Paris and join her. Meanwhile we would write to each other daily. I had no idea at that time just how long one could be detained by the responsibilities of a large estate. So often it seems wealth has a faculty of enslaving people no less than poverty.

Immediately after Taya's departure I plunged into the work. Countless legal documents needed disposal, as well as numberless decisions to be made. I had no experience in these matters and but for Maradze, would never have worked myself from under the dreadful pile of papers. Maradze's patience knew no bounds. He spent many hours trying to explain things which must have appeared childishly simple to him. More than once I felt like throwing everything into his lap and running away. But each time I realized how the fate of many people depended on my seeing the thing through. Literally hundreds of families had depended on Grandfather's generosity for full or partial support. I was determined to make sure this support would not be discontinued or interrupted.

Then finally the last document was signed and I was free. That very night I took a train for Batoum, then the first boat to Marseilles. Maradze came to Batoum to see me off and as I shook his hand I thought I detected a slight mist in his eye.

But I had no fear. Samourzakani and its people were in capable and honest hands.

"Toot… Toot… Toot!"

Now we passed the suburbs of Paris with all its factory buildings, mills, barracks, warehouses, narrow streets, shabby brick houses and skeleton trees black with soot. The fog had lifted but now a fine drizzle continued to obscure my window. Finally the train started to lose speed as it picked its way between the endless rows of drenched freight cars and clanging points, all the while tooting its whistle. Then it was time to start taking bags down from the luggage rack, which I did with Erast's help. Suddenly the compartment darkened as the train entered the covered débarcadère of the Gare de Lyon. Then we jolted to a halt.

We had arrived in Paris.

There followed the sounds of hurried steps in the corridor,

excited voices, snatches of laughter. Someone knocked at my door and a round red face with a walrus moustache peered inside.

"Porter Monsieur?"

Without waiting for an answer two husky men invaded the compartment and, much to Erast's consternation, started unceremoniously to gather up our luggage. Erast jerked my large suitcase away from one of the men.

"No!" he cried angrily in Georgian. "Don't you dare touch the Prince's things with your dirty hands; thieves!"

If it had not been for my energetic interference, the scene could easily have turned violent. But even with all my explanations and entreaties Erast flatly refused to let the men go. Eventually the three of them departed together, Erast between each porter, holding them firmly, determined to defend my property to the very last.

The platform teemed with people, both new arrivals and those meeting them. All around I saw embraces and exclamations of delight. Children jumped up and down in excitement. Porters loaded with bags, suitcases and trunks, pushed their way rudely through the crowd as luggage trucks rumbled along the platform. Hôtel agents loudly proclaimed the superiority of their establishments. Grease-smeared men in blue blouses, oilcans in their hands, swarmed under railway cars hammering at brake-boxes and wheels. Dapper policemen in black capes – that made them look more like villains in a melodrama – did their best at maintaining law and order in an utterly disorderly scene. I could see that Erast, still holding onto my porters, was becoming increasingly panic-stricken in the pandemonium.

And then I saw Taya.

She stood beside one of the station's structural steel pillars, a tall and beautiful young woman in a simple black coat, skirt and petite hat, her eyes scanning the crowd. For a moment my heart stopped beating; then it leapt wildly. The dreary station suddenly transformed into a palace of delight, and the pandemonium, a kind of dancing. Either I had forgotten how beautiful she was, or she had simply grown more radiant since our parting in Tiflis. At any rate I was not prepared for the shock of seeing her and found myself struck speechless. Once again, just as in Tiflis, an instinctive and paralysing fear shot through me like cold lightning. What if I should lose her; what if she should disappear; what if I or she should die first and we became parted?

"Taya, Taya, my only Taya!" I wanted to shout at the top of my voice, but instead I said nothing at all, just stood there looking at her, afraid to believe my luck or my own happiness.

Finally Taya spotted me, but she too did not speak or move. But a half-smile touched her lips and her eyes seemed momentarily to shine.

I felt an overpowering desire to run forward and throw my arms around her, sensing she felt the same. But instead we stood before each other neither moving nor saying a word. Finally she gave me her hand in a grey kid glove. I took it gently, held it as if taking possession of a brittle item of jewelry, then we started to walk down toward the exit. Erast and the porters trudged behind us. Back in Tiflis, then on the train and boat, my mind had rehearsed the many things I wanted to tell Taya the moment we met. In fact so many things, a lifetime would hardly be adequate. Yet now, holding Taya's delicate hand, I could not find a single word to say to her, even to save my life.

It was a strange phenomenon. Not actual speechlessness; I could talk to others, indeed I hired two fiacres, one for Taya and myself, another for Erast and our luggage. Without any difficulty I gave the drivers the address of the apartment leased for me by Monsieur Renault, Grandfather's agent in

Paris. I paid off the porters and dismissed them. I spoke to Erast but still found myself dumbstruck with Taya, even though I racked my brain for any item of conversation. There are simply no words in any language to express what we felt at that moment. I assisted Taya into the carriage, and we set off.

That morning Paris was in one of its moods – and that mood was anything but gay. The rain had stopped, but the naked chestnut trees shivered in the chilly wind and the wet cobblestones clacked in protest at our horses' hooves. Taya sat beside me and her arm touched mine. But she kept her face turned away, looking out the window.

We rode this way for some time.

"Look...!" she exclaimed suddenly. This was the first time I had heard her voice in many months. "Blue sky, look over there!"

True enough, a microscopic patch of blue had appeared over some far away chimneys. But this fact was suddenly of no interest to Taya and me. Her words had finally broken the spell. Suddenly she turned toward me, our eyes met, and we laughed spontaneously. Then we started to talk, hardly listening to the words or even understanding them, just delighting in the sound of our own voices sounding together. Now we were finally back, united in our old intimacy and our youth.

"Taya, I'm here!"

"I know."

"You don't understand. I'm here to stay."

"I know."

"I'll never leave you again as long as I live."

"I know."

"Taya... How did you get out of school today?"

"I just walked out."

"But Taya... you'll be in trouble!"

"Yes. Mademoiselle Nocq will be furious. I don't think she has ever been young."

She laughed, I laughed and all of Paris laughed with us. The sun broke out momentarily and flooded the cold streets with a layer of beaten gold. It was just so good to be in Paris, alive and in love. It was so wonderful to look into Taya's laughing eyes and know that those eyes would be there until the end of time.

"How's everything in Tiflis?"

"There is no Tiflis without you."

"Silly! How's Maradze?"

"Well. How's Mademoiselle Agathe?"

"Don't you know?"

"Know what?"

"She's on her way to Georgia to marry him now, this minute."

"No!"

"Yes. You must have passed her somewhere in the Mediterranean."

"Incredible. Maradze hasn't said a word to me about this."

"He couldn't because he doesn't know. This is Mademoiselle Agathe's idea of a grand surprise. You ought to have seen her trousseau; nine trunks, each as big as the Opera House!"

We laughed and again the whole world laughed with us.

The apartment prepared for me by Monsieur Renault turned out to be charming, a large studio-living-room downstairs, cosily if a little gaudily filled with imitation Louis XIV furniture, and two bedrooms upstairs facing the courtyard. However, thoroughly liveable, and we arrived to find everything ready for habitation. A fire crackled in the fireplace and the curtains had been opened. The old concierge had been warned of my coming and gone out of her way to prepare the rooms. She explained that Monsieur Renault had left for Toulouse on business, but would see me the moment he arrived back in town. In my mind I thanked fate for business which made people go to Toulouse. I felt in no mood to see

Monsieur Renault that morning or discuss the affairs of Grandfather's properties in France. I wanted this day for just myself and Taya.

Erast brought our bags upstairs and fell to unpacking them, carefully checking every article as he lifted it out. Although he had hovered over my luggage like a hawk all the way from Batoum, he insisted on making sure all my belongings were accounted for – and nothing in the world would prevent him.

Meanwhile Taya and I sat downstairs before the fire, gazing at the dancing flames. The nervous tension of our meeting had vanished and a sublime peace descended in its place. We felt content just to sit silently together and drink in the state of happiness. I took Taya's hand and stroked each long sensitive finger as though a rare treasure – as indeed it was. Then I reached into my vest pocket and, extracting an antique gold ring, gently slipped it over her third finger. Taya looked at the ring, turning it around with her thumb. It fitted her finger perfectly.

"Where did you get it?" she asked.

"It was my grandmother's," I answered. "It was made for her by a goldsmith in Samourzakani before she and Grandfather were married. Now it's yours, Taya."

"Thank you," she said quietly, still looking at the ring and sliding it round her finger. "It's very lovely. I will always wear it – out of school of course. We are not allowed to wear rings in class."

"When do you finish?" I asked.

"In May, that is if I don't fail geometry."

"Then we can marry in June."

"Yes," she said thoughtfully, then added without a shade of self-consciousness. "Early in June will be perfect. I've thought we might go to Lausanne and be married in Mother's room. I don't know if that's possible... according to church rules, but I know that it would make her very happy."

"How is she?" I asked.

Taya did not answer, but a shadow passed over her face. I was immediately sorry to have asked.

"Does she know... about you and me?" I asked, to change the subject.

"No," Taya said.

"NO? You haven't told her you're to be married, Taya?"

Taya looked at me and two impish lights flickered in her eyes.

"How could I, when you have never proposed?"

"Taya!"

"You have never even told me that you liked me, Shota."

"I love you!"

"That's the first I've ever heard about it."

That was true. Never before had either of us used this word; it seemed so small when compared to our feelings. Now, when finally uttered, it sounded so weak and trite I felt almost ashamed. I took Taya's hand and kissed it several times with great tenderness.

"I will write to Mother tonight," she said without attempting to remove her hand. "I will explain everything and ask her blessing. She will be very happy."

"I hope she will like me," I said.

"She will."

For a moment the fire crackled silently and cheerfully before us. Then Taya spoke again.

"Why are we so lucky, Shota? Why out of all the people in the world has God chosen us for such happiness? We are no better than others; there are people who are kinder and wiser than we, and probably more deserving... Why then have we been given so much? Sometimes it frightens me. Sometimes I fear I might wake up in the morning and discover all this has been just a beautiful, mad dream."

"This is no dream," I said.

"Incredible luck, then?"

"No," I said. "This is not luck. What has happened to us was inevitable because we are really one person and our souls one soul. We have never been apart. Even before we saw each other you were I and I was you. We were one soul, one mind, one heart. Nothing could have kept us separated, just as nothing can ever separate us. No one can create such a unity if it wasn't already there, and no one can break it once it is. We have nothing at all to be afraid of, Taya."

"One soul, yes..." she said thoughtfully. "It's true. I've felt it ever since that day we met in Aunt Manya's garden... Do you know that I could feel everything you felt, and seemed to know all your thoughts?"

"Of course. Don't you remember those wonderful conversations we held while riding silently through the park?"

"It's eerie," she said a little nervously, rising to her feet and running her fingers through her silky hair. "I'm hungry, Shota. Don't you think we should go out and celebrate our engagement? I'm dying for a brioche."

"A noble thing to die for," I said, catching her sudden change of mood. "Where shall we go?"

"Now that's a problem. There are only five thousand places in Paris that sell brioches at this hour."

"Wonderful," I said. "I'll be ready in a second."

I ran up the stairs three at a time, almost knocking Erast off his feet. While making myself presentable with the help of my assistant – who complained bitterly that one handkerchief had been fiendishly stolen from the bottom of my brown suitcase – I heard piano music drifting up from the living room. Taya was playing something I had never heard before – simple, sad and languorous, with an unmistakable gypsy air. The melody seemed to capture me, hold me in its spell.

"What's that?" I called from the top of the stairs.

The music stopped. "What is what?" she called back. "That tune."

"Oh... an old romance Mother used to hum when I was a girl. For some reason I could never forget it. Are you ready?"

"Almost. What's its name?"

"I don't know. Hurry up, I'm getting lonely down here."

"I'm coming..."

The sun was shining brightly when we left the house. A fresh wind had swept the grey morning clouds from the sky and now it sparkled blue and turquoise. No town can change its mood as quickly as Paris, and no people can catch that changing mood as quickly as the Parisians. Driven temporarily off the streets by the rain, now they again overflowed the boulevards, talking, laughing, jostling as that high-strung, high-spirited crowd so characteristic of this fine city.

I wanted to hail a passing fiacre but Taya said no, she preferred to walk. So away we strolled, arm in arm, through the city streets, boulevards and squares, without any plan or design. The crisp wind bit at our cheeks, sudden gusts whirled the coats around our bodies. But oblivious to such details we lost ourselves into the spirit of the town and our delighted mutual observations. Once, crossing a wide boulevard, we were nearly run down by a private carriage and received a sharp rebuke from the fat coachman. But we only laughed in response. Nothing at all mattered beyond our being together and alone on a late windy morning in this most wonderful of all cities. We walked on and on through its streets like two soldiers marching toward a great victory.

We must have wandered for some time, because when we finally stopped before a watchmaker's shop to stare at a monstrous bronze clock in the window, we suddenly realized it had passed noon.

"Have we had breakfast?" Taya asked, looking at me bewildered.

"I don't know," I said helplessly. "I don't think so."

"Neither do I. What about our brioche?"

"We can still get it, but I have a better idea. Let's have lunch instead. Look over there, the Café de la Colombe; just the place for us!"

We crossed the street to the restaurant. The pavement tables were all occupied by people sipping coffee or wine and noisily discussing ways to get even with the Germans for the Sedan débâcle.

"Let's go inside," I ventured. "I don't want to share you this morning with the whole street."

"Then let's go upstairs," said Taya.

"I don't think they open the upstairs room before dinner," I said.

"We can ask."

We found the maitre-d'hôtel and asked. He shook his head. No, the upstairs room was closed. He was sorry but there was nothing he could do.

However, after accepting the banknote I slipped into his hand, his outlook suddenly brightened. He stopped a passing waiter.

"François," he said, "Mademoiselle and Monsieur here are going upstairs. You will serve them up there."

"Very well," said the waiter and rushed on.

The maitre-d'hôtel took us upstairs and seated us at a small corner table near the window. The room was completely deserted, the tablecloth crisp and the view from the window magnificent.

"The garçon will be here presently," said the maitre-d'hôtel.

"We are not in a hurry," Taya assured him.

However, François, the waiter we had met downstairs, appeared almost at once. He was a man of about thirty with reddish hair and laughing blue eyes, and, perhaps because we were so completely happy ourselves, we thought him remarkably friendly. He took an active part in our selection from the menu, strongly recommending some dishes and warning us against others in an excited whisper – like a true French gourmet. Finally, after some intense discussion, our order met with his approval and he departed.

"I wonder what he thinks of us?" Taya laughed.

"I don't think he cares," I said. "He has his own life and it is every bit as important to him as ours is to us."

That was all we said. After this we just sat looking at each other, and found we could not look long enough. Our carefully selected food eventually arrived, only for us to discover our appetites had been banished by the intensity of our emotion.

Several times François peered into the room, saw that our food lay practically untouched on our plates and disappeared. Finally he returned again but this time stayed. We noticed he now wheeled in a wagon-tray carrying a wine bucket. The dark green neck of a champagne bottle looked forlornly out from the crushed ice. He pushed the wagon straight over to our table then started to twirl the bottle expertly between his palms.

"You have made a mistake," I told him.

A mischievous smile spread over his freckled face. "Oh, but François never makes mistakes Monsieur."

"You have this time. We've not ordered any wine."

"That is perfectly true Monsieur. I have the great honour to offer this little bottle to Mademoiselle and you with my sincere compliments."

"Oh no," I protested. "We couldn't…"

"Ah, but you would do me a great honour Monsieur," he said pulling the bottle out of the ice and wrapping it in a napkin, "a great honour."

"But why do you do it?" asked Taya, completely bewildered.

"Ah, now you are asking me a question Mademoiselle. I

have worked here for over ten years and been watching people's eyes, Mademoiselle. And in all these years I have not seen more happiness than today in the ten minutes of looking at your eyes. If there were more eyes like that in the world people would rise with a song in the morning and go to bed laughing."

The cork popped out of the bottle and the foaming wine flowed into crystal goblets. "May I wish you a long life and may happiness grace every second of it, Mademoiselle, Monsieur..." he said, placing the glasses before us.

For a long second we were speechless and then Taya took her glass. "Thank you," she said, her voice low with emotion. "I shall never forget this."

Taya drank and I drank, still overcome by the drama of the event. François watched us with a grin. Then he unclasped the shining badge from the lapel of his coat and placed it on the table cloth before Taya.

"May I offer you this Mademoiselle as a token of good fortune?" he said respectfully. "It has brought good luck to me since I received it last spring. I've married the woman I loved and two days ago she gave me a fine son who, with God's help, will aid in bringing Alsace-Lorraine back into the fatherland."

Taya took the badge.

"Thank you," she said. "I will carry it with me always wherever I go. And some day I shall come back here and tell you how it worked."

"It will work Mademoiselle."

François refilled our glasses, threw the napkin over his arm and departed, leaving us alone. For a few moments we sat motionless and silent, Taya staring at the shining badge in the palm of her hand.

"Nine," she said finally, as though answering her thoughts. "My lucky number... I will always treasure this,

Shota, above all the jewels I may have. It has been given from the heart and it will always remind me of you, our love, and the happiest day of my life."

She opened her handbag and dropped the badge inside.

"Let's eat!" she said eagerly, snapping the bag shut and setting it on the table beside her. "We must not disappoint François. He's the first friend we've met since our betrothal and I know it's a wonderful omen!"

We attacked our food with gusto. The wine, so graciously proffered to us by François, had whetted our appetites. We enjoyed every bite, pausing only to look into each other's eyes and laugh some more.

Seven

ISHTVAN IRMEY

MADEMOISELLE Nocq's School for Girls carried a Europe-wide reputation for its scholastic excellence and educational techniques. Discipline was exacting and rigidly enforced. The pupils were not allowed to leave the grounds without written permission from the Directress, and Mademoiselle Nocq was never generous with this, especially to girls whose families lived outside Paris. It is small wonder then, that after Taya's escape from school on the day of my arrival we didn't see each other for some time. I received a hurriedly scribbled note from her saying she was 'in jail.' When finally she succeeded in getting out with a formal permit this time, she told me what had happened. Mademoiselle Nocq had questioned her sternly on her return. When Taya refused to explain her actions she was told that a second violation of the rules, no matter how small, would result in automatic expulsion. That was a dire threat for Taya because her mother took great pride in the fact that her daughter would soon receive her diploma.

"It would kill her," Taya said desperately. "It really would. We must be patient, Shota. Ten more weeks and I'll be free as the wind. But for these miserable weeks we must suffer. I know you understand."

I did. I well knew Taya's tremendous devotion to her infirm mother and respected and loved her for it. We discussed the situation and Taya told me she could be reasonably sure that by exerting her full charm on Mademoiselle Nocq, she would receive permission to leave school every Sunday afternoon after church, just for a few hours. But that was all. So we had to content ourselves, after waiting the whole week, with these few hours. A maddening condition, but we both agreed we'd no other option.

Even correspondence wouldn't work as pupils were forbidden to receive letters from anyone but their parents. My letters, which I had written from Tiflis, were all addressed to Poste Restante and Taya collected them once a week. But now even this proved impossible.

Nevertheless we found a way to overcome Mademoiselle Nocq's draconian restrictions – via a form of mental telepathy quite beyond the good lady's power to prevent. Each week we would select a book from the school library and every night at exactly the same time, read the same pages – Taya in her dormitory in school, I in my living room by the fireplace. The theme of the book served as a medium between us. We amazed ourselves at the success of this home-grown mesmerism. In the end we found we could transmit actual messages to each other. When we compared notes on Sundays we discovered our telegraph worked almost as well as the one invented by S. B. Morse.

But then we were highly sensitive youngsters with our intuitions still finely tuned. Many things impossible to others we found easily within our grasp. This I only realized more fully later in life. But during that interlude in Paris we never took our strange powers seriously. Our technique had been no more than a clever ruse to get round Mademoiselle Nocq and an excuse for our feelings of delight when it appeared to work so well.

As for our weekly meetings, every one turned into an enchanted adventure. But one in particular stands out in my memory. It happened on a Sunday afternoon late in March. I met Taya as usual in front of the small flower shop a few streets from the school. The air still carried a slight nip but the first signs of spring were already there. A new and invigorating wind now drifted across the city streets with a whole new range of delicate scents.

Taya took both my hands in hers. Then her face lit up with such a blinding smile I felt I was being dazzled by a brilliant light from head to foot.

"Guess what!" she cried.

"You passed geometry."

She snatched her hands away. "How did you know?"

"You're forgetting our conference last night; the twelfth page of 'Toilers of the Sea!'"

She laughed. Never before or since have I heard such laughter as Taya's. It filled itself with a complete abandon and echoed back all the warmth and charm of her whole being.

"I nearly died of surprise. Yesterday morning they announced the results, and without any warning. No warning...! When I sat that exam I had been so completely nervous I couldn't tell a circle from a triangle. And the theorem Mademoiselle Duval gave us... you should have seen it! Only a truly warped mind could think up anything so preposterous. But when I opened my notebook do you know what I did...? I thought of you."

"And...?" I asked.

"And I was the second in the whole class to finish. Mademoiselle Duval nearly fainted when I placed my note book down on her desk. I've no doubt the shock kept her awake all night!" Again her laughter sang out and she linked her arm with mine. "Do you know what that means, Shota?"

We were walking along the street toward the river.

"What?"

"It means I'll finish without any trouble. I was afraid that I'd be forced to take a summer course before getting my diploma. But not any more! In four weeks I'll be a free woman, sir, ready to marry you... if you'll have me."

"This is SO sudden," I said. "Please give me a little time to consider."

"Better hurry. I have several meritorious offers. Let's go to 'Chez Moi!' I want to celebrate!"

'Chez Moi' in spite of its egocentric name, was a very modest place across the river which we both liked. Tiny, secluded and usually deserted on Sunday afternoons, it also served the best pastries in town – or so it seemed to us. The proprietress, Mére Charbon, a huge kindly woman, had a weakness for Taya. We often stopped there for an hour or so.

She greeted us with a huge smile that seemed to split her face so completely it was a miracle it stayed in one piece. "My children...!' she exclaimed ecstatically. "I hoped you'd come today. I've baked Napoleons that would have saved the poor Emperor himself had he known about them at Waterloo."

"What, used them to shoot at Wellington?" Taya exclaimed, planting a kiss on the woman's cheek. "Then let's have them! Today is our celebration, a feast."

So we had a feast. We had Napoleons, cream puffs and coffee. I even drank a glass of wine. The pastries were divine and the wine bad, but I drank it with a relish that would have done honour to the court of Le Roi Soleil. For now the last obstacle between us and our future had been removed. Taya's weakness at mathematics, especially geometry, had threatened to keep her locked away in that school far longer than would be right.

But now our entire life spread before us like a golden carpet. Mentally we were already treading it. I wanted to sail around the world for our honeymoon but Taya held out for Egypt. So Egypt it would be. We would spend the winters in Paris and the summers in Samourzakani, where Taya could organize summer schools for the peasant children, based on the advanced methods of education taught at Mademoiselle Nocq's.

"Have you heard from your mother?" I asked casually.

"Yes," Taya said, "I had a letter yesterday."

"Anything new?"

"No. She still thinks she should meet you before giving her consent... but it's a mere formality, Shota. You don't know Mother. She's the grandest, the most considerate person in the world and she'd do anything at all to make me happy. You'll fall in love with her the moment you see her. But she's terribly careful about anything that touches me...You can't blame her, can you?"

We were ready to leave and I helped Taya with her coat.

"No," I said, "of course not. Where shall we go?"

It was now dark and the ribbon of gaslights reflecting on the river gave the impression of a fairy tale in progress over on the opposite bank.

"Let's go to Montmartre!" Taya suddenly turned to me. "I've never seen those terrible places. But it's all right now, I'm practically a married woman."

"Aren't you afraid you might run into Mademoiselle Nocq dancing with an Apache?"

Even Mére Charbon roared with laughter at the idea.

We decided to make an evening of it. First we visited several of Montmartre's more touristy cafés, none of them at all disreputable, but to Taya still a great adventure. Her eyes glowed, her cheeks flushed and never before had I seen her so animated. This was her evening and she would enjoy it to the very last.

It was growing late by Mademoiselle Nocq's standards when we finally arrived in 'Szeged.' This Hungarian restaurant is famous across Europe for its wine cellar and no less exquisite gypsy music, played by the gypsies themselves. I had heard many reports about 'Szeged,' but never visited it. When I suggested it as our last port of call, Taya agreed readily.

The place itself turned out to be small, set in a basement at the bottom of a steep and winding stairway. Deliberately modest in its décor, the management had obviously made no attempt at embellishment. The restaurant was so dimly lit as to be almost dark and its arched stone ceiling gave it the feel of a medieval dungeon or torture chamber. But this atmosphere was obviously all part of its stock-in-trade. The tables were placed along the walls in small recesses, carefully arranged so that each, although separated from the others, afforded a clear view of the low-lit estrade in the room centre. The table surfaces were of dark wood, left bare without tablecloths or napkins to give the appearance of a cheap tavern. But actually 'Szeged' was one of the most expensive restaurants in Montmartre. Champagne was obligatory and its price exorbitant. As we entered I found myself at a loss to understand what made so many people come and spend whole nights in such a seemingly unloved and melancholy room.

A waiter dressed in a gypsy kaftan and boots led us to a table and inquired whether we wished for anything else beside champagne.

"Why is the place so empty?" I asked.

"It is very early Monsieur. By three o'clock in the morning every chair will be taken. People come here when they leave the other places – and this week they will come from afar."

"Why?"

The waiter's face assumed an expression of reverence. "Ishtvan Irmey is here, Monsieur."

"Who is Ishtvan Irmey?"

The waiter looked at me disbelievingly. "Ishtvan Irmey is one of the greatest artists there is, Monsieur. People follow him all the way from Budapest and Vienna."

"What does he do?"

The waiter's patience was clearly wearing thin. "He plays the violin Monsieur, that is when he is in a mood to play. No one knows when he will play. People just sit and wait, and hope. On some nights he doesn't play at all."

I told him that we wanted nothing but champagne and he left. "Now we know that Ishtvan Irmey is a man and he plays the violin," I told Taya. "As for the rest, that remains to be seen."

Taya did not answer. The dungeon-like atmosphere had obviously affected her. She looked sad, troubled, even a little frightened. She pulled her brown coat more closely around her neck and shivered nervously.

"Do you want to go, Taya?" I suggested. "It's getting late and you're due back at school by eleven."

"Yes," she said, "I want to go, Shota. It's so damp and sad in here."

I stood up looking round for the waiter to pay for the ordered champagne. But at this very moment a tall and ancient looking man approached our table. He wore a red shirt fastened by a cord tipped by two dangling tassels. Under his arm he carried a violin. But his face, I shall never forget. Long and almost completely lifeless, its parchment-like yellow skin stretched over prominent cheekbones and a large aquiline nose, while above it the hair was completely snow white. Only his eyes showed any life at all – shining back with a fierce, almost fanatical glow from under the bony eaves of his brows. Standing there before us he had the appearance of an early Christian martyr dying on the cross, yet somehow still defiant, unconquered.

He looked at Taya for a few seconds, then with a quick movement of his arm threw the violin to his shoulder and the bow flashed past his face. The first notes of a haunting gypsy melody floated into the room. Slowly I sat down, transfixed. Instantly I knew why people followed this man across Europe. No one played the violin quite like Ishtvan Irmey. Indeed it hardly sounded like a violin. All the sorrow of existence, its pain, misery, indeed its very soul seemed trapped inside those plaintive sounds. And was it good music, was it bad...? All I could say for certain was that Ishtvan Irmey was indeed a very great artist.

I looked at Taya. She sat motionless gazing into space, her eyes completely entranced by the power of the violin. The waiter bringing our champagne had also stopped still, just a few steps from the table.

Finally the last tragic note of the violin died away under the arched ceiling. But we sat on in silence, afraid to move a muscle lest we break the spell cast by this ancient instrument into the dingy, modern room. Finally Taya passed her hand over her eyes.

"Beautiful!" she whispered in Russian.

A smile slowly appeared on the old man's lips, which then spread across the network of wrinkles that amounted to his face. That smile seemed to breathe a sudden life into what until then had seemed no more than an ancient wax mask. Now we found it transformed into a finely chiselled and kindly face.

"I thought you were Russians," he said softly, struggling with his Russian words. "That's why I played for you... Your people know how to listen to music – with their souls."

The waiter, who by now had come back to life, placed glasses before us and opened the bottle. Ishtvan Irmey turned to him and spoke in some guttural gypsy dialect and the waiter nodded. He quickly brought another chair and the old man sat down, placing the violin on the table beside him.

"You speak good Russian," Taya said politely.

"I have been to your country," he nodded. "Many, many years ago when I was young and strong I travelled with your gypsies through the cold northern woods and empty Volga steppes, learning their songs..."

"Taya," I said, "perhaps Monsieur Irmey knows the song you played the other day, remember? The one your mother used to hum... It follows me everywhere."

"Oh..." Taya said, hesitating.

"I know many songs," the old man smiled at Taya. "They sang good songs when I was young."

"Please, Taya," I begged.

"There is no piano here..."

"Just hum it..."

Taya wrinkled her forehead trying to recapture the tune in her mind, then began to hum softly. As she did so a strange change came over Ishtvan Irmey's face, as if it suddenly reflected the activity of some deep and personal struggle. Taya stopped momentarily but the old man nodded impatiently. She started humming again. Slowly, half unconsciously, Ishtvan Irmey lifted the violin to his shoulder, then began to play again. He knew that song and he knew it very well. He proceeded to play with such feeling that Taya and I could only hold our breaths. Other people in the restaurant stepped out of their stone cubicles to listen, also completely captivated. The tune he played was of such a beauty that when the old man finished and placed the violin back down on the table, no one even dared applaud. Looking at him I noticed a tear had appeared on the parchment of his cheek.

"That's an old song," he said quietly, trying to wipe away the tear before we noticed, "an old, old song. I have not played it… oh, for perhaps fifty years. Sometimes people ask for it, but I never play it."

"Why?"

"I promised a friend."

There was a short pause.

"What is it called?" Taya asked.

"I don't know its name… I heard an old gypsy sing it one night many years ago. Its words say that only once in our lives do we meet our true love, just once and no more… Never more. It's a truly sad song."

I offered him wine but he refused politely, asking instead that the waiter bring him strong tea. Meanwhile the restaurant gradually filled as new groups kept arriving, mostly well-dressed men and women in furs. As they passed our table they cast quick glances at Ishtvan Irmey. Some even smiled at him, but he paid no attention, just kept sipping his tea.

"Will you play again tonight, Monsieur Irmey?" Taya asked.

"I don't know," he said "I can play only when my soul moves me. One can't make good music with the hands alone... That would be dead music, like everything made by hands alone."

By now Szeged was starting to hit its usual nightly stride. Bottles popped and waiters hurried to and fro with wine buckets and trays. A gypsy string quartet set up on the estrade and shortly afterwards started to deliver their usual repertoire of beautiful melodies, now sad, now exuberant. Ishtvan Irmey listened silently for a while then shook his snow-white head.

"Good musicians…" he said. "Very good. But they play with clever hands, they don't understand and they don't feel. And it's such a simple secret."

"What is it?" Taya asked.

He looked at Taya for a moment then smiled again. "Many

people come to me and ask, 'How do you play, Irmey? Teach us.' Good people, fine musicians. 'Look,' I always tell them, 'Look, this is how I play.'"

He crossed himself devoutly. Both Taya and I were puzzled.

"Nobody understands," the old man continued. "They think old Irmey is making a joke. But this is the only way to do things that live." He repeated the gesture. "First forehead and heart – which is mind and soul together. Then shoulders – which link to your arms and thus connect all three. Mind alone – dead; soul alone – good but directionless; arms alone – worst of all because without mind and soul they act not knowing the consequences and that way create things that hurt others."

"How true," Taya said, clearly impressed.

"I was a bad musician until an old monk in the Moscow woods taught me this secret. After that only one man ever properly understood it. 'Irmey,' he would say, 'you don't play the violin; you pray.' 'Yes,' I said, 'I pray all the time.' 'Pray for me,' he said, 'because I don't understand my life or God's ways.' And I played for him the song I have played for you tonight. I have never played it since he went away, until tonight."

He paused looking away, immersed in memories.

"When was that?" I asked.

"Oh, perhaps fifty years ago in Budapest. He was a fine young man, big and muscular with a soul as large as the world. He became like a son to me. He would come and I would play this song for him over and over. He sat and just listened with an aching heart, because although rich and handsome he was also an unhappy man. It seems the one thing he craved the most in life he could never have. 'Play Irmey' he would say, 'play it again because still I don't understand.' I would play and my soul would weep with his."

The old man stopped, lost again in his memories. By now the restaurant was completely full. Every chair had been taken and the waiter passed our table several times giving us impatient glances. I told him to put another bottle of champagne on our bill and leave us alone.

"What happened to this man?" asked Taya softly. The old man put down his cup. "One night just before dawn, he came to my room in Buda across the river. As usual I got out of bed and took down my violin, but this time he told me to put it away. 'Don't play your song any more, Irmey,' he said and put his arm around me, 'because now finally I've understood. Now I know it's true that once only in life does a man meet his true love, but it is not true that he can ever lose it; nor should he weep about it. Your song is a lying song, Irmey. Never play it again. A man can never lose a love that is so deep. Perhaps in this life yes. But what is this life, Irmey? Look, I'll show you what this life is!' He took his watch from his pocket and opened it up. 'Look, Irmey,' he said. 'This is what unhappy people call life. Little wheels, little springs, two silly little hands. That is why people suffer in this world, because they watch these hands, instead of the hand of God which points to the only real way to live.' With that he threw his watch straight out of the window, impetuous boy!"

Ishtvan Irmey chuckled softly at the memory.

"And then?" Taya asked.

"And then he went home. He gave me a lot of money, more than I had ever seen before, and just never came back. He must be well on in years now. Let me see… He was maybe twenty and I forty… That would make him seventy now… or seventy-two perhaps… a good, very good age for a man," he added pensively.

Taya and I exchanged glances, touched to hear him reminisce about the time when he was seventy, which to him now must appear the prime of his life.

"Did he ever marry the woman he loved?" Taya asked.

"That I don't know," he replied. "I never saw him again. But he was a happy man when he left my room."

He rose, picked up his violin and tucked it swiftly under his arm. I found it difficult to believe this tall agile man could be as old as he claimed.

"Good-night children and God bless you," he said pulling out a massive gold watch of obvious great vintage. He pressed a button on the side and the gold cover flicked open to reveal its face. "Look," he said, "I found the watch the next morning in the brambles outside the window and kept it... It still runs well and if I ever see him again I will give it back. It's an expensive watch."

Taya and I looked at the watch, then we looked at each other. Engraved on the back of the cover was the d'Iberios coat-of-arms and Grandfather's initials, 'P. d'I.' no mistake about it. I had seen these initials a thousand times in Tiflis and Samourzakani. Taya too must have noticed them on the linen and silverware.

Ishtvan Irmey snapped the cover shut and slipped the watch back into his pocket. "Good-night," he said again cheerily and walked away with a measured step that seemed in complete defiance of his age.

Silently I paid the bill and silently we walked out of 'Szeged.' I hired a fiacre and we rode all the way to Taya's school without speaking. We never even said good-bye. I just kissed her hand and she touched my brow with her warm, soft lips. I watched her disappear through the monumental portals of Mademoiselle Nocq's establishment, then asked the coachman to take me home.

In front of the house I saw the tall dark figure of Erast loitering on the pavement.

"What are you doing here?" I asked, amazed at this nocturnal vigil.

"There is a man in our house," he told me excitedly.

"A man? What man?"

"I don't know. He wears a black overcoat."

"Have you been drinking?"

"Yes, but very little. He came tonight and I told him you were not at home. 'Le Printz ne pas maison,' I told him, but he must not understand French because he went straight into the living-room and sat down. I watched him from the hall, but he must have seen me because he didn't take anything, just sat and sat. So I locked all the doors and came downstairs to wait for you. He can't get out."

It was by far the longest speech I had ever heard Erast give at one time, and the most unusual. I did not expect any visitors, having intentionally kept my presence in Paris a secret from my few casual acquaintances – specifically to avoid the necessity of social activity. It could not be Monsieur Renault because Erast knew him.

I opened the front door and walked upstairs, Erast at my heels.

"Do you want me to stay outside and catch him if he tries to escape from the window?"

"Give me the key Erast," I said rather curtly.

I opened the door of my apartment. From the anteroom I could see a man seated comfortably in the chair near the fire-place. I don't know why but this irked me slightly, possibly because Taya had sat in this chair the day I came to Paris and slid Grandmother's ring onto her finger.

The man heard my footsteps and abruptly stood up to face me. He was young, blond, handsome, and impeccably dressed. Everything about him shone with an absolute correctness; his height, posture, gestures and manners.

"Prince d'Iberio, I presume?" he asked with a neat little bow. His French too, was precise and correct to the point that you immediately knew him to be a foreigner.

"Baron Helmouth Kluge von Klugenau," he introduced himself, "Third Secretary of the Russian Imperial Legation in Bern."

We shook hands and I asked him to sit down. He did so, carefully straightening the creases of his trousers around his knees. Clearly he was a fastidious young man.

"Forgive my intrusion into the privacy of your home at this hour," he said, "but I carry a personal message of considerable importance to you I believe, and I am leaving Paris in two hours. In an hour and forty minutes," he corrected himself, glancing at his watch.

"A message?" I said, "from whom?"

"Madame von Lemberg."

That was the name of Taya's mother and my interest quickened.

"Yes?" I asked eagerly. "And what is the message, Baron?"

"Madame von Lemberg requests the pleasure of your presence in her residence at Lausanne at your earliest convenience, to discuss certain confidential matters of great importance."

"Yes of course... I've contemplated a trip to Switzerland in the near future... In May, perhaps."

"Madame von Lemberg is in extremely poor health," the young man said as steadily and politely as before. "Any delay at all may prove to be unfortunate. If I may say so, Prince, an immediate trip would be the only proper course under the circumstances."

I stood up nervously and paced the room, thinking. I knew I ought to see Taya's mother at once; that it was undoubtedly something extremely important for both Taya and myself. Yet before leaving I wanted to see Taya and speak to her. As if reading my thoughts, the young man spoke again.

"It is Madame von Lemberg's express wish that her

daughter not be informed of this suggested meeting. She wishes to keep the matter strictly confidential because otherwise the proposed conference might not achieve the desired results. Madame von Lemberg knows that she can rely on you to respect her wish."

"Of course, Baron," I said.

The young man rose, picked up his overcoat, hat and gloves, and bowed again. "Good-night, Prince. It was a distinct pleasure to make your acquaintance, I assure you."

He clicked his heels and walked out, while I resumed my pacing. Thoughts raced through my mind. Evidently Madame von Lemberg had an excellent reason for wishing to see me alone and immediately. Quite possibly her health had deteriorated to such an extent that she realized she might not survive until the time Taya and I came to Switzerland in May. But then why did she want to see me alone and not Taya, or Taya and me together? All my guesses were futile. I had no choice but to go. The day was Monday. That gave me more than sufficient time for a quick trip to Lausanne and back before my tryst with Taya on Sunday. Perhaps Taya's mother was wise after all, not wishing to cause her daughter any undue anguish during these last few weeks which were so crucial for her school work.

"Erast!" I called.

Erast materialized in the doorway as though by magic.

"Pack my bags, Erast. We are leaving tonight." A wild hope lit his jet-black eyes. "Going home to the mountains?"

"Different mountains, Erast. Come on man, hurry!"

I clapped my hands and Erast ran up the stairway like a frightened mountain goat.

Eight

DOCTOR BAUER

I opened my eyes.

I had not the slightest idea where I was, who I was, or what had happened to me since the day I was born. I did not even know whether I was alive or dead. The only thing of which I was conscious, and very acutely, was my head. It felt enormous; like a great cast-iron ball filled with pain. But the pain was not stationary. It splashed from side to side like water in a tub as it tipped back and forward, surging and recoiling and threatening to spill out over the brim.

I tried to lift my head but that proved hopeless.

The moment it moved thousands of steel mallets hit the sides of my temples in unison. I succeeded, however, in rolling it to one side. Only then did I discover I was in bed. By squinting my eyes and gradually finding focus I began to discern things around me. It looked like a conventional hôtel room: A dressing table with a mirror; a chest of drawers; a secretaire; a few chairs; two windows with drawn curtains. On the walls several coloured gravures showed heroic scenes from the Napoleonic wars.

In a corner of the room the bony figure of a dark-haired

man stood without moving, like a wax effigy. His eyes were open and fixed, without life. For a moment I struggled with consciousness, trying to fit this apparition into any possible scheme of reality. Then the man blinked and I remembered... this was Erast and he was alive. That meant I was alive too and Erast was with me, which suddenly seemed very comforting.

Not wishing to attract his attention I shut my eyes again. The pain immediately splashed around my head again, but now fragments of consciousness started to appear within the dark liquid. They floated like pieces of broken ice on an autumnal river. Some then stuck together momentarily to form little floes, until the storm of pain again wrenched them asunder.

"I must wait," I thought incoherently. "My mind is going to freeze over sooner or later. The pieces of ice are growing larger and larger all the time."

That was true. I suddenly found myself watching a furry brown bear, the favourite toy of my early childhood, float by on a large floe of consciousness. The animal looked at me with his glossy button eyes; gave a smile with his permanently stitched red mouth. He had been a dear old friend and I reached out towards him with my imaginary hands – only to find the vision dissolving away to drop me back into the black pool of pain.

"I must be patient," I told myself, still manoeuvring through the mental maze of broken ice. "I am in Paris... Or am I in Paris? No, I am in Lausanne... but why am I in Lausanne? I have come here to see someone..."

Suddenly a sharp new vision sprang out of the confusion. This time it came as a pair of human eyes gazing straight into mine, wide and intense. These two pale grey beacons cut right through my brain and scoured at the very bottom of my soul. So powerful was the impact of those eyes that they left me stunned. But finally I managed to shake myself free, then with great difficulty sit up in the bed. Immediately the pain was back splashing itself all around the room.

"Erast!" I wanted to shout. "Erast!"

But my tongue was so dry, hot and swollen I could hardly move it in my mouth. In the end I produced nothing more than a hoarse whisper.

"E...rast..."

Erast blinked, slowly came back to life, then walked over to my bed.

"Erast... where is she?"

"Who?" asked Erast.

"You know who, my Taya... What day is it today? Sunday?"

Erast took a glass of water from my night stand and pressed it to my lips. "You drink some water," he said with an awkward tenderness. "Water is good... cold and fresh."

He held my head gently as I took several thirsty swallows, my teeth chattering on the glass. Then I pushed Erast's hand away.

"Drink some more..." Erast begged me. "You were very ill last night again... Very, very ill. Iller than ever before."

I dropped my head back on the pillow, suddenly completely exhausted. Once again the pale grey eyes floated back out of nowhere to confront me. But this time they would not be shaken off. They just stared straight back. My headache was ferocious, but now quite insignificant beside the new feeling of despair and gnawing emptiness suddenly flooding my entire being. If only the pain could be sharper, I thought, a million times more severe, then perhaps it could drown out this unbearable torture...

I pressed my teeth together until every bone and muscle in my mouth screamed out with pain. I shut my eyelids with such force that I saw red circles shooting in all directions. I wanted to disconnect my brain from all sense of reality, to sink back into the dark oblivion from which I had just emerged. But most of all, I wanted to break out of the prison of those eyes and their pale grey stare.

But it was too late. Consciousness had moved in, taken possession of my brain and started to give orders. Horrible maggots of thought began swarming through my head and there was no way to stop them. One picture after another thrust into my mind, each one cruelly clear and vivid. Soon the terrible sequence of events, beginning with the young Baron's visit to my Paris apartment, started passing across my mental screen in a vile and triumphant parade.

Erast and I had left Paris early the next morning, cut across half of France, crossed the Jura mountains at Pontarlier and arrived in Lausanne toward evening. I left Erast at the hôtel where he preferred to stay and guard my belongings, hired a phaeton and drove the two or three kilometres out of town toward Madame von Lemberg's house. Eventually I arrived at the secluded villa by the lakeside.

A white-clad woman, apparently a nurse, answered the door and told me curtly that Madame von Lemberg could see no one. However, when she heard my name she reluctantly asked me to come in, then seating me in the living room, departed to announce my arrival. The room was conventionally and tastefully furnished in satin and pastel-blue, edged with gold braid. At first I found myself impressed, but slowly the sensation changed, then darkened as I started to pick up on an imperceptible aura of restlessness pervading the house. All my life I had been highly sensitive to the atmospheres surrounding people and objects, although I tried to convince myself they were the mere products of an over-active imagination. But the longer I sat in Madame von Lemberg's living room, the more vividly waves of nervous apprehension started to rise up and attack me from all sides.

Outside the day started to die away slowly beyond the distant mountains. Pale shadows crept across the room and gathered in the corners. From where I sat I could see a life-size oil painting hanging over the fireplace. It showed a strikingly beautiful young woman – undoubtedly Taya's mother in earlier days. The physical resemblance between the two women was obvious. The same delicately sculptured features; the same radiant eyes; the same sensitive slightly curved mouth with the suggestion of a smile touching the corners. But while Taya's entire personality spelled out kindness and charm, the woman in the portrait seemed to possess an aura of indomitable will and strength. Whoever painted that picture had given his subject a soul of steel.

"Madame von Lemberg will see you now."

I stood up and followed the nurse out of the room. My heart pounded as I sensed myself stepping toward a moment of great destiny. Indeed, had I not been preparing for this meeting from the first day I met Taya? We walked along a dimly-lit corridor to the door of Madame von Lemberg's bedroom. The nurse opened it. Inside the room was almost dark; the tightly drawn curtains sealed away any traces of the fading daylight outside the window. In the glow of a flickering sanctuary lamp I could just discern the white shape of a bed near the wall. The air was warm and carried a faintly medical odour. In those days tubercular patients were still carefully shielded against cold air and any sudden drafts.

"Let me put on the light," said the nurse in a low voice.

I stood by the door while the woman walked over to the table nearest the bed and started fumbling with the lamp.

"Good evening, Shota…"

It was Taya's voice. My heart leapt. But while that voice carried exactly the same warm, melodious quality, it sounded very faint as if coming from behind a wall. For an instant I looked around trying to find Taya, but of course, Taya was nowhere to be seen.

"Come here…"

The voice originated from the direction of the bed. I took some faltering steps toward it just as a bright crown of flame suddenly caught the wick of the lamp and cast a flare of light out across the room.

Then I saw Madame von Lemberg.

I will never forget that first impression. Propped against a carefully arranged heap of white pillows was the head of the woman who had once posed for that portrait in the living room. But every trace of that triumphant, vigorous beauty had departed. The cruel ravages of disease had sucked every hint of colour from that face, and so completely it seemed virtually transparent. I found it difficult to understand what kind of power still kept this dead woman alive... unless it was her eyes. Enormous and out of all proportion to that small withered face, they burned back at me like two flaming candles. They possessed a pale grey intensity that seemed not so much to look at an object as to penetrate right through it. Now I was that object and suddenly felt myself very ill-at-ease under their scrutiny. I would have given a great deal just to be able to turn away, but they held me securely in an unblinking grip.

"Leave us alone Anne," she said to the nurse, without taking her eyes off me.

I could hear the nurse moving away behind. The soft creaking of the door told me that Madame von Lemberg and I were now physically alone in the room. I say 'physically,' because I could feel another presence in there with us – the Angel of Death. His existence was so palpable and strong that cold shivers started running down my spine.

"Shota," she spoke slowly, "I can call you by your first name because we are in no way strangers. We have a great and precious thing binding us – our mutual love for Taya and nothing, do you hear me, nothing can be allowed to interfere with it or with Taya's happiness."

Her voice was low, in fact barely audible, but it still contained such a fierce and uncompromising conviction that every word seemed to cut straight through me like white-hot steel. The effect was then redoubled by the presence of those two piercing eyes and their insistence that not one word or syllable go unheeded.

"Listen carefully, Shota. Taya's welfare and Taya's happiness are the only two things that matter. Everything else is secondary and unimportant. I will not die knowing that her future is in any danger. I want you to know and understand this."

She spoke as though she had absolute control over time and her own death, and that I had no right whatsoever to question any of her words. Then I completely understood what had kept her alive so long – a fanatical, if not pathological love for her daughter. She was determined to remain the eternal guardian of her every step for as long as protection was needed.

"I do," I said.

"Good! Then you will also understand why I will never allow you and Taya to marry each other."

The phrase struck me so brutally that for a moment everything turned black before my face. But within this blackness the two pale grey eyes continued to stare fanatically into mine. They seemed to grow and grow in size until they filled my entire field of vision. I made one last desperate effort to break free.

"Why?" I demanded.

"Because you are ill."

"I'm not," I protested. "My doctor says that my case has completely arrested."

"It will strike you again."

"It will not!"

"How do you know? It may strike you tomorrow and kill Taya along with you. Is that what you want? Answer me."

Her words were passionate and cruel and carried such a force they suddenly snapped my will. Our brief duel was over. Her eyes gripped me more tightly and held me as if in a vice. They seemed to punch holes in my brain and force her words through, one by one.

"There is no escape, I should know. Thirty years ago I was pronounced well by every specialist in Europe. Today I am dead. You think you are well today. But the illness will strike you again, swiftly and treacherously at the moment you least expect it. And even if it spares you, it will strike your children and your children's children, perpetuating horror and death into other lives. No. You will never, never touch my Taya."

Up to this day I do not understand the power wielded over me by that dying woman. But whatever it was, it crushed me completely. All the arguments and protests forming in my mind collapsed. Suddenly I believed she was right; that tuberculosis was a hereditary disease; that I was a doomed man as well as a selfish scoundrel for attempting to visit my own tragedy upon the woman I loved. However, it should also be noted that at this time tuberculosis was still a largely misunderstood condition, accepted as a dreaded and fatal disease, accompanied by all kinds of superstitions and fears in the popular mind. Perhaps this explains why Madame von Lemberg's words, when delivered with such force and magnetism, managed so totally to overwhelm me. They also awakened a fear in me for Taya's own health, which I had hitherto not considered. And this was probably my downfall.

Sensing my weakness, she drove on relentlessly.

"You will never marry Taya. You will not marry her because she would never go against my wishes, and also because you really love her. I do not ask you to stop loving her. That I know is impossible. I do not ask you to forget her. That too is beyond your power. But I do demand in the name of God and your love, that you let her live her life in happiness without bringing additional horror into it. She has already had well enough of that. It is not an easy demand but you must and you will comply with it, Shota, because that is the only thing you can do if you wish to face your conscience and your God again. I am close to Him now, very close, and I know that He is watching you this very moment, waiting for you to give your answer to a dying mother."

Her words shattered my will completely, then seemed to fill me with a strange exaltation and the strength to face up to whatever doom awaited me, fairly and squarely.

"He is waiting, Shota."

It was that new inner strength that spoke when finally I forced my lips to move.

"I am ready," I said.

Her eyes went through me like iron needles.

"Kneel down."

I did, now completely in her power.

"Now repeat my words. On my honour and in the presence of God I do hereby promise to spare Taya's life and happiness by dropping out of her existence for ever and not attempting to see her again for as long as she or I remain alive."

I repeated this pledge word by word, and shocked myself by the deadness in my voice. Although I knew that for all practical purposes my life was over, I did not care any longer.

"You may now rise."

She was no longer talking to or arguing with me. She simply told me what to do and I followed her orders. I stood up and looked back into her eyes.

"Tomorrow morning you will go away, Shota, to some place where there is no danger of your meeting Taya again. But before you go you will write her a letter. In this letter you will tell her that your love was a mistake; that you release her from all her promises to you; that you ask her to forget you and not make any attempts to see you again. You will post this letter not from Lausanne, but from some other place, because our meeting tonight must remain a secret as far as Taya is concerned. That would be easier for everyone and give her a chance to find peace and happiness quicker than if we do it in any other way. Do you agree with me?"

"Yes," I said. I no longer cared what I said or did. All I wanted was to flee that room and never see those eyes again.

Slowly she sat up in bed – a desperately difficult task for her – then blessed me with the sign of the cross. Somewhere deep in my soul, I resented this blessing, but still remained obedient and motionless as though riveted to the floor.

"If the nearness of death gives one's blessings any added power," she said slowly as if reading a prayer, "I am giving all of it to you, Shota. I am blessing you for your great love for Taya and I pray that God will give you solace and comfort in your ordeal. God bless you, Shota."

She sank back to her pillows in utter exhaustion and for the first time shut her eyes. Only then did I notice the wetness all over my body. The collar of my shirt was sodden and small trickles of perspiration ran down my face. I backed away towards the door, found the knob and slipped out of the room. Groping my way along the dark corridor I managed to steer myself out of the house. The nurse attempted to speak to me, but I never understood a word she said.

The phaeton was still waiting outside, its driver peacefully asleep. I put some money on the seat and walked away. I wanted to be left alone and set off along the road, staring at the distant lights of the city flickering over the darkened lakewater. Then I stopped. For a fleeting moment a wild protest rose up in my soul like a waterspout. I felt a sudden urge to rush back and wrest away my promise from Madame von Lemberg; tell her that the demands were utterly unreasonable, inhuman, and beyond my powers of compliance. Bitter words flashed through my mind. But only for a moment. Then the pale grey eyes appeared out of nowhere and the rebellion evaporated. Again some strange power took hold of me and pushed my feet away from that house, from the place where I had left behind everything I held most dear in life.

I walked for a long time, my mind and soul a blank. No feelings, no thoughts, just endless dull pain. I must have wandered for many hours, because when I finally stopped I'd reached the point of complete exhaustion and my legs felt numb. I looked around. The street was dark save for the lights of a small café shining out from the far side of the road. The sound of music drifted out from behind its closed door. Desperately needing to sit down and rest, or else drop down right there on the street, I dragged myself across the pavement to its door. At this late hour the tavern was almost deserted. Two or three men sat in dark corners brooding over their drinks. Two lovers, a young man and a plain-looking girl were locked in a tight embrace, oblivious to the world. The music came from a concertina played by a nimble-fingered Italian with a mournful, drooping moustache. At that moment he played a sentimental Neapolitan love song with much feeling. Candles burned low on the tables and cast swaying shadows across the room.

I sat at a small table near the door and gazed at its candle flame as it rose and fell like the quick curtsies of a girl arriving at her first ball. It took me some time to notice the proprietor pressing his enormous friendly stomach up against the table edge.

"What would be your pleasure, Monsieur?"

I brought out a gold coin and put it on the table.

"I want some paper and a pen."

The proprietor lifted his eyebrows, "Ah, Monsieur is a poet. A noble thing. I myself have been consorting with both Thalia and Erato…"

"That is fine." I said miserably. "Please take the money and leave me alone. I am very tired."

The fat poet took the coin and walked away. I sat for a while staring at the curtseying flame. The old musician finished his song and started another, just as sentimental. Soon the proprietor came back with paper, pencil and also a small glass of greenish liquid.

"Nothing courts the Muses better than a glass of good absinthe," he said with a professional flair.

"Thank you."

He walked away and only then did I remember why I had asked for paper. It inspired another violent rebellion in my soul. But this outburst, too, was quickly stifled by the thought of Madame von Lemberg's eyes. I started to write the words, "Dear Taya," and immediately crossed them out. I tried again and again but found myself unable to compose a single sentence.

Mechanically I sipped the drink with its sweet taste and smell of wormwood. Not liking it much I put down the empty glass but then experienced the sensation of warm waves suddenly flowing through my body. With them the pain seemed to ease slightly. I ordered another drink. The tavern soon became brighter, the music sweeter and I began to feel as if several swarms of bees had started to buzz around my head. Then suddenly the pain was all but gone.

I ordered another drink. This time the proprietor brought a half-filled bottle and placed it before me. Perfect; now I would be left alone. Feeling braver I started my letter again and this time the words flowed more readily. After several more false starts and a good many more drinks, the letter was finished and I read it through.

"Taya dear," it said. "I have gone away from Paris and out of your life because it is God's will that we never see each other in this life again. I beg you to trust the wisdom of His judgment and submit to it with reverence and humility. In the name of our immortal love, I beg you not to search for me in our present mortal existence, but to go through it happily, without bitterness or regrets, knowing that it is but a fleeting moment in the timeless way that lies before us, and that when our time comes to start another journey, I shall be waiting for you with all my love. But until then, let God's will be done on earth as it is in heaven. Shota."

I slipped the letter into my pocket and felt strangely relieved. Then I finished off the bottle. Or… was it another bottle that I finished and in some other place… Because after that night in that tiny tavern, there were so many other bottles and so many other places.

The next morning I left Lausanne, but wherever I journeyed my anguish and pain followed faithfully. There were nights and days, bottles and splitting headaches, then new nights and days, new bottles and new headaches. My life became nightmarish but mercifully unreal, and eternally permeated by that sweetish green liquid. Only this seemed to kill my pain and erase from my mind the presence of those pale grey eyes. Then gradually the sequence of time started to disappear. Days became nights and nights days, forever accompanied by my faithful Erast begging me to stop drinking. I experienced jolting train rides, drafty hôtel rooms, then new bottles and new headaches with periods of blissful blackness in between. I dedicated my whole life to the pursuit of these periods of black oblivion.

"…Prince Shota… Oh, Prince Shota…"

Someone was gently shaking me by the shoulder sending ripples of pain through my head. Angrily I opened my eyes and saw Erast's face set against the ceiling.

"Get me a drink," I said.

"The Doctor is here," said Erast almost guiltily.

I propped myself up on my elbow only to be momentarily

blinded by a new and sudden headache. Then as its wave recoiled and the mist before my eyes dissolved I realised I lay in the same hôtel room I had been in before, only this time the curtains were up and I could see pieces of pink cloud floating across the sky.

"How do you feel, my boy?"

I recognized Doctor Bauer; the same wonderful Doctor Bauer I had known and loved since childhood. To me he always resembled King Henry VIII. A big jovial man with black shovel-like beard tacked around his fleshy face and a pair of thick silver-rimmed glasses set low on his nose. He sat in the chair beside my bed. As usual he wore a black frock coat, grey trousers and boots with elasticated sides, and on his face an expression that blended medical severity with an infinite kindness.

For a moment I failed to understand why Doctor Bauer could possibly want to sit in this room. Then came a sudden flash of memory. My brain had been operating in flashes ever since I had started on the absinthe. I remembered that Doctor Bauer had come here to Monte Carlo some time earlier, summoned by a frantic telegram from Erast. He had found his address among my letters then managed to compose the telegram in his peculiar blend of Mingrelian and French. At any rate the good doctor had arrived to examine and test me almost every day – much to my annoyance.

Now I found myself annoyed again.

"I feel awful," I told him very honestly.

"Did you drink again last night?"

"Yes Doctor," I said with irritation. "I did and I'll do it again. What's more, I'm perfectly happy doing it."

"You're killing yourself, my friend," said the doctor flatly. He had a real talent for colourless and dispassionate speech. "You're destroying your nervous system."

"Suppose that I am.... I'm not drinking for my health, Doctor. I appreciate your interest in me and I'm very thankful for everything you have done, but there is no point in pretending. I know what I'm doing and I don't require medical attention. I'm killing myself as you say, because I can't do anything else. I've been cursed with an incurable disease since birth and I see no point in trying to prolong my existence by artificial means."

Doctor Bauer took off his glasses, extracted a large handkerchief, then exhaling on the lenses started to polish methodically. This purely mechanical action was the routine the doctor always followed when confronting a psychological illness or condition.

"You have no disease at present," he said gently. Then after a moment of deliberation added. "Whoever told you that tuberculosis was incurable? If it is incurable, I have wasted a good many years of my life."

The pain in my head suddenly stopped.

"Isn't it?"

"Not according to the latest medical research. The incurability of tuberculosis has been disproved just as conclusively as its supposedly hereditary properties."

"You can't mean that, Doctor..." I whispered.

"Your test is negative. That proves beyond any shadow of doubt there are no tubercular processes anywhere in your system."

"But the test might be wrong... Yes, it might all be wrong..." I said, horrified at his words.

The doctor breathed on his lenses and began to polish again, refusing to let himself be disturbed.

"The Koch's tuberculin test is now accepted by the profession as the most reliable agent in the diagnosis in all stages of phthisis. That is point number one. Point number two is its clinical manifestation. In your case it is quite clear. You have gained weight since your trip home; your heart is good and your lungs are free from any foreign bodies or growths. This is especially remarkable in view of the, shall we say, strenuous style of life you've pursued of late. All this proves rather conclusively that in your case we have a pronounced example of the complete cure. It is not just an arrested development, as I thought before, but a cure. Today you are as sound as any man under the sun."

The room started to whirl before my eyes. "But Doctor... it may strike me again, may it not?"

The doctor looked at me through his perfectly clean lenses, then removed them again and started to polish.

"It might," he agreed philosophically, "but the chances of recontracting the disease in your case are no larger than for any human being in an average state of health. In fact they may even be smaller. Your system has proved its ability to cope with tubercular processes in a rather remarkable way, and..."

But I didn't listen any further. Instead I leapt from the bed with such an agility I knocked the glasses clean out of the doctor's hands. They flew across the room but fortunately landed on a padded chair without damage. In two more energetic jumps I made it to the adjoining washroom then looked at myself in a mirror – not a pretty sight. Several days' growth of stubbly beard needed urgent removal and brown pouches hung under my eyes. But the headache was gone without trace and I never felt more vigorous in my life.

"Erast!" I cried in a voice which made the pendants of the chandeliers vibrate. "My razor and brush... quickly! And start packing those bags... We're going right back into life and at full steam!"

Poor Erast must have thought the green poison had finally completed its work. Gingerly he handed me my razor then stood back in the doorway clearly baffled, watching me work the shining blade energetically up and down the stropping leather.

"Maybe you want a drink?" he ventured.

"No. But by all means have one yourself."

Erast crossed himself and stepped forward into the room. Now he understood the change in my mental condition. I soaped my face and started to shave. Meanwhile Doctor Bauer took Erast's place in the doorway, trying vainly to strike up intelligent conversation.

"At any rate my friend, I strongly advise you to cut down on alcohol…"

"I don't want to see another bottle as long as I live! What date is it today?"

"The fourteenth. Alcohol has a pronounced tendency…"

"What month?"

"May… to lower the resistance of your system, as well as…"

"Then Taya's already out of school… Erast! Run downstairs and tell them to get a compartment for us to Lausanne!"

"…as well as permeating your brain cells, clogging capillary vessels, and…"

I grabbed Doctor Bauer's shoulders so suddenly and roughly that his glasses slid down to the tip of his nose.

"You're coming with me, Doctor! We are going to see a dying woman who, in her delusions, is ruining the life of her own daughter! You're going to explain everything to her, coldly and scientifically. She will understand because she loves her daughter and because she is the victim of terrible misinformation. But we must hurry because unless she releases me from my pledge I'm hopelessly bound and helpless to avert a great tragedy involving two people desperately in love… Erast!" I roared noticing him still hanging around in the background. "Didn't you hear what I said? Three express tickets to Lausanne… in three minutes. One… two… three… hurry!"

Erast jumped out of the room. There followed the loud rumble of feet as he ran down the stairs.

Nine

THE BARON

WE arrived in Lausanne during a torrential downpour. The sky was leaden and a cold wind sent sheets of an icy rain slashing against the trees and buildings. Nothing at all suggested spring. The weather seemed to have skipped straight to November.

We left Erast at the hôtel, took a cab and drove out to Madame von Lemberg's suburban villa. Doctor Bauer sat next to me cold and uncomfortable in his long black overcoat, but I never even noticed the weather. All my thoughts were focussed on Taya and our imminent meeting with her mother. Now I had no fear of this meeting, Madame von Lemberg, her eyes or her strange powers. I felt fully prepared to meet and challenge them all.

Since it was also quite possible Taya had now arrived in Lausanne and I was still bound by my word not to see her, we decided that Doctor Bauer would enter the house first, speak to Madame von Lemberg and explain that all her fears about my health were groundless. Meanwhile I would wait in the cab ready to join the conference at a propitious moment. Then we would conclude the matter once and for all.

The thought that I would see Taya again, perhaps in a matter of minutes, filled my entire being with a tingling anticipation. In my mind I ran through all our wonderful times together so that I failed to notice the moment our creaking carriage came limping to a stop outside Madame von Lemberg's house.

"Here we are," said Doctor Bauer, buttoning up his wet overcoat.

"Do you remember everything you have to say Doctor?" I asked nervously.

"Yes."

"Good luck."

The doctor opened the door and stepped outside. I wiped the misty window of the carriage with my sleeve and watched him wade through the mud to the front gate. It happened to be unlocked so he walked straight up to the front porch. As he reached for the bell handle my heart pounded. Someone would answer the bell, the nurse, or perhaps even Taya herself. Seconds passed and Doctor Bauer remained standing on the porch, his hands in his pockets. Then he reached for the bell and rang again. Still no answer. Finally the doctor looked around bewildered.

Unable to keep myself in the carriage any longer, I jumped out and hurried over to the doctor.

"Well?" I asked.

"There's no answer," he said looking at me through glasses now genuinely in need of a good wiping. "Perhaps they're still asleep. It's very early…."

He pointed to the windows. All the curtains were tightly drawn so I then pulled at the doorbell and heard it clang inside. We waited again for what seemed like an eternity. No response. I rang again and again. Cold fear started to rise up inside my body.

"Come," I said.

We circled the house sloshing through the mud, and eventually found the back entrance. I tried the knob. The door was locked but with no bell to ring, I beat on the glass with my knuckles and with increasing strength. Still no response.

"Perhaps they are out..." suggested the doctor.

"How can they be out when Madame von Lemberg is bedridden?" I countered sharply as if the doctor himself had been the cause of our predicament.

I resumed my banging.

"What do you wish, Monsieur?"

The voice addressing us came from directly behind our backs. Turning round we found ourselves staring at an old man wearing a ragged cape. He stood on the cobblestone path that led through the backyard toward the servants' quarters. An unlit pipe stuck out of his mouth – which he chewed.

"We want to see Madame von Lemberg."

The man made a hopeless attempt to relight his pipe in the rain. Finally satisfied the task was impossible, he jammed it into his pocket.

"You're in the wrong place," he informed us laconically.

"This is her villa..." I protested.

"That is true, Monsieur, but she's no longer here."

"What do you mean?" I asked rather stupidly.

"She died."

Everything inside me went numb. Furious thoughts flashed through my brain. This was a terrible, perhaps even fatal complication. How could I now secure the release from my pledge? How could I go to Taya and explain anything? Then I heard Doctor Bauer's voice. It seemed to come from far away.

"When did she die?"

The old man contemplated the question, then began counting on his fingers and mumbling. "Must be about ten days or so... Maybe eleven. She died the day after her daughter was married."

The doctor's glasses slipped down his nose and fell into a puddle. He made no attempt to pick them up.

"They had the wedding in Madame von Lemberg's room..." continued the watchman retrieving the glasses. "Just the priest, the bride and the groom. Your glasses, Monsieur."

"Whom did she marry?" asked Doctor Bauer, mechanically taking the glasses.

"I have her new name and address inside. They left for Paris yesterday and gave me the address in case there are letters. You wait here..."

He walked away toward the servants' quarters. Only then did the full import of the disaster crash down on me, and with a soul-crushing force. I felt my knees give way and clutched at Doctor Bauer's wet coat sleeve.

"Let's go," I said, making a supernatural effort to pull myself together.

"Wait," the doctor mumbled, shaking raindrops from his eyelashes. "You can write to her..."

"Please... please, Doctor!"

I pulled at him and he followed me, wading through the ankle-deep mud. We made it to the waiting carriage and drove away before the old man could return.

Unpredictable indeed is our human psychology, because at that moment the only thing upsetting me was the thought of Taya carrying another name. It seemed utterly monstrous and filled me with a blinding rage so powerful it pushed aside every other thought and emotion.

Doctor Bauer sat beside me nearly as devastated. He seemed ashamed of his inability to alleviate my agony in any way. This was a man who had dealt with human suffering all his life, but always the physical variety. There at least he knew the cause and chemistry. But with me he confronted something no physical science could engage or explain – an acute cancer of the soul, probably the most wretched of all human afflictions.

Finally the silence inside our jolting cab became so suffocating he could endure it no longer.

"Perhaps you should see her..." he ventured haltingly.

"What for?" I asked sharply.

"To explain..."

"Explain what?"

"I don't know..."

"Stop!" I ordered the driver. We had entered the outskirts of the now thoroughly dismal and rain-soaked town. The cab drew to the curb and stopped. I opened the door, climbed out and cast a quick glance at Doctor Bauer. He looked so crestfallen and helpless that despite my agony, for a moment I felt sorry for him.

"I'll be all right," I told him.

His eyes were colourless and forlorn behind his mud-spattered glasses.

"You will drink..." he said with anguish.

"I don't know," I said.

"May I come with you?"

"No."

"Please, Shota. I will not speak. I promise you."

"No Doctor. I must be alone for a while. Go home and don't tell Erast anything. He would be too miserable."

I slammed the door and started to walk. The fiacre followed me for a block then drove on and disappeared into the haze of rain.

I walked and walked. Time ceased to exist and everything around me lost meaning. Before long my overcoat, shirt, underclothes were drenched through and I felt the hostile cold water creeping down my body, working its way into my shoes. But I kept on walking. The sky turned dirty brown and lights began to ignite in the windows. Still I kept walking. It felt like an instinctive if hopeless attempt of the body to shake free from its own diseased soul, before the poison of mortality finally arrived to kill us both.

"Look out!"

I turned, caught a tiny glimpse of an enormous and grotesque horse's head bearing down on me like an avalanche. Then came a ringing impact; fistfuls of bright sparks – and finally a complete, measureless and all-consuming blackness.

An ambulance brought me to the municipal polyclinic and Doctor Bauer was summoned at once. I arrived there unconscious but without any broken bones. When I failed to regain consciousness the next day and my temperature started to rise, Doctor Bauer decided to move me to the private clinic of his friend – one Doctor Maurice Verne in the town of Vevey some fifteen kilometres out of Lausanne. There, assisted by Doctor Verne, he diagnosed my condition as concussion of the brain aggravated by developing double pneumonia.

Both Doctor Bauer and Erast made their home at the clinic and from that point on Doctor Bauer fought incessantly and heroically against the death that constantly tried to snatch me away. On the nineteenth day the pneumonia was finally brought under control and I regained partial consciousness – according to the case notes which Doctor Baner kept religiously throughout my illness.

All these things I learned only much later. The nineteen days mentioned in the doctor's records did not exist for me. From the moment I glimpsed the horse's head, to the second I became conscious of the white painted ceiling of Doctor Verne's clinic, I had been dead in every material sense of the word. No remembrances, no feelings, emotions, visions or subconscious impressions of any kind imposed themselves. For all practical purposes that blackness could have continued for nineteen more days, nineteen years, or for ever without affecting me in any way. It was the first time in my life I had tasted pure timelessness, except possibly in certain moments of deep sleep. But even in sleep the hours are alive with dreams. My nineteen-day night had been completely black and devoid of life in every aspect.

I clearly remember my first impressions at the end of that black period – as purely physical experiences experienced through a brain still enveloped in a kind of numbness. I saw the white ceiling, then I heard Doctor Bauer's soft voice telling me I had been ill but was now recovering.

Then came a first, very brief, glimpse of consciousness, but I drifted back into the darkness almost at once. I crawled into it again happily and snugly, knowing that I was alive, that it was now but a temporary refuge.

The period of purely physical resurrection then continued for some time. I would become conscious now and then, even speak to Doctor Bauer and Erast, only to drift back into my black lair for another short hibernation. Never did I escape or want to escape my state of mental and emotional torpor. I was alive. This was the single sustaining thought or rather sub-impression dominating my mind and body during those brief snatches of reality.

But I also improved physically. I could see it in Doctor Bauer's eyes. They grew quieter and more relaxed. Erast, too, was slowly assuming his usual appearance. No longer the haggard, unshaven Erast I had seen during my first flash of consciousness. Now his tie hung straight again and I even noticed one day he had trimmed his craggy moustache. This was the surest sign of all I had come out of immediate danger.

Then one night consciousness returned to my brain not as an occasional visitor but a permanent tenant, and with a full suitcase. But that suitcase was indeed formidable. It contained not only a complete sense of time, place and identity, but also brimmed with a lifetime of memories with all their pains and despairs.

I remember how it happened. I awoke and for a while lay motionless, wrapped in my usual sense of animal well-being. A tiny shaded light dimly lit the room from over in the corner. I could see the white bedside table covered with medicine bottles, the white blinds on the windows, the white spread on my bed and the white-clad figure of a nurse, asleep in a chair. The only sound in an otherwise dead silence was the barely audible ticking of the watch pinned to the nurse's chest. But it was that feeble ticking that proved my undoing. The sense of time abruptly flooded back into my life as a terrifying sensation. Suddenly I understood that I had been ill, probably for a long period; that time had steamed ahead without me as I remained behind in my illness; that Taya had been alive all this time; that I had not heard anything about her for some time... time, time, time...

Once that sense of time had taken possession of my brain it would not relinquish its grip, even for a second. The thought-maggots restarted their triumphant march through my head. The anguish which I had shaken off on the rain-swept street under the horse's hooves tumbled back in an instant, just as sharp, if not sharper than ever before. In one second I remembered every aspect of my life and concluded with absolute certainty that the greatest tragedy of all was that I remained alive. I could not possibly live without Taya and now it seemed I could never have her.

The thought was so utterly crushing it produced a reflex reaction in my body. It tensed all my muscles, stretched itself out under the blanket, pressed my teeth together and emitted a groan. The groan brought the night-nurse, a middle-aged woman with greying hair, out of her trance. She hurried her long, severe face over to my bedside.

"What time is it?" I asked in a loud whisper. It was my first conscious question since the accident – and perfectly symbolic in its pointlessness.

The nurse glanced at the watch on her chest. "Three thirty-three. Time to take your medicine."

"Where am I?"

"Doctor Verne's clinic."

"What city?"

"Vevey."

"How long have I been here?"

"About four weeks. Open your mouth, please."

"Where's Taya?"

"Who?"

"Where's Doctor Bauer?"

"He'll be here in the morning. Open your…"

"Is Erast here?"

"Yes, asleep in the next room. Your mouth please. You must take your medicine."

I took my medicine. It was bitter and the nurse gave me some warm water which I drank.

"Go to sleep…" she said with motherly concern. "You must rest."

If I only could! I dropped my head back down on the pillow and shut my eyes, but it was only a pretence. Thoughts slashed through my mind like meteors, leaving long flaming trails. I had lost Taya. She too had submitted to her mother's power. I would never see her again. I had not the slightest justification to remain alive, yet God in His unfathomable way was pulling me away from the supreme oblivion which He had given me briefly to taste. Or was it Doctor Bauer's skill? Whatever it was, I wished passionately to return to the blissful Nirvana, so recently lost. But I was a religious man and could not accept or justify my own violent self-destruction. That to me was a violation of the Divine Will which created and maintained the processes of physical life. But was it not permissible for a man who had lost his will to live, to submit to a natural death by just ceasing to struggle against it?

I remembered how Grandfather once told me of his conversation in Tiflis with Elena Blavatsky – the simple Russian
housewife who launched into the Western world with esoteric
teachings from India and seemed to possess great knowledge
and powers. "Your teachers appear to hold that physical life
is evil," Grandfather told her. "If so they should approve of
self-destruction as a means of entering the higher plane of
existence." "Yes," the extraordinary woman had answered,
"but only if the man in question has lost all his ties with this
world. If for instance he should die prematurely because he
has forgotten to take nourishment – simply forgotten, mind
you – then his death, even though suicidal by nature, would
not constitute a breach of Divine Laws."

I felt certain I had no ties with the world. I reasoned that
death, by the simple process of forgetting to get well, would
be a Christian solution to all my problems. A perverted idea
perhaps, but at that moment it gave me comfort and I drifted
back to sleep in a slightly happier frame of mind.

I woke in the morning and saw Doctor Bauer again. For
the first time since my accident I was able to speak to him
logically. He warmly congratulated me on my tremendous
physical tenacity that had pulled me through this, the gravest
crisis in my life.

"I would never have been able to save you, my friend,
without it. It was a sheer miracle and defied all medical
prediction."

I also spoke to Erast, even joked with him. But despite all
this, underlying everything I felt the complete absence of any
will to live – exactly as before.

From that day on the course of my illness changed
remarkably. I ate all the food given me, took every pre-
scribed medicine and followed every rule – but still kept
slowly deteriorating. The deterioration, however, was purely
physical because my spirit and mind remained strong and

clear. But my body no longer resisted the illness – not so much because of my premeditated plan, but due to some strange apathy which enveloped my entire being. I simply ceased to care.

At first Doctor Bauer accepted the turn of events as a temporary relapse. But when I failed to rally and continued to deteriorate he became alarmed. He tried various methods of treatment but without success. Finally, when my physical condition reached its very lowest ebb, he called in two eminent physicians from Lausanne. The three doctors discussed my case at length. One admitted to a complete inability to diagnose my condition; the other said he possessed a certain preparation which had worked wonders in cases like mine. It was decided that Erast would go to Lausanne with the doctor and bring back the medicine. It was late evening when the concilium finally broke up and the two doctors, along with Erast, departed for Lausanne.

Doctor Bauer remained in my room seated at my bedside, thoughtfully wiping his perfectly clean glasses. Never before had I felt so ill. My mind was giddy, my temperature high and my breathing laboured and irregular. I also showed signs of approaching delirium. Certain things about the room began to disturb me. I kept glancing at the door afraid that at any moment it would start opening. My bedspread appeared annoyingly disarranged. The medicine bottles on the table looked back at me with an innate hostility.

Finally Doctor Bauer placed his glasses back on his nose. "Shota," he spoke in a low voice, "Erast will bring the medicine which Doctor Weiss praised so highly. We are going to try it of course. But no medicine in the world is going to help you if you don't wish to live."

"Why Doctor…" I started to protest feebly.

"Don't say anything now, Shota," the doctor interrupted gently. "Let's discuss this matter in the morning when you have thought it over. There is nothing very wrong with you physically. But all your vitality has disappeared. After all, pills, tinctures and powders are only ammunition with which to fight an illness. What good is ammunition when there is no will to fight? Now you must rest. I shall give you a pill that will make you sleep."

Doctor Bauer's pill did indeed make me sleep, and quickly. But during the night I awoke again. The room was empty; the dim night light burned in the corner and everything remained utterly quiet. Even the ticking watch seemed to have stopped; then I realised the night nurse must have stepped out. I felt very weak, my forehead was wet with perspiration and chills ran up and down my body. My temperature must have been high as my vision was blurred and I felt a pounding in my ears.

I lay motionless, trying to think. Doctor Bauer's words had affected me strongly. They shocked me into the realization that I was actually dying – otherwise the good doctor would not have spoken as he did. Usually he only sought to encourage his patients. The thought of actual death frightened me briefly. It was one thing to accept it in one's mind, quite another suddenly to see it staring you in the face. For a moment my physical self, or what remained of it, revolted against my spiritual surrender. But I managed to suppress this mutiny quite easily. Very well, I reasoned, I am dying. But is this not exactly what I want? Should I not simply wait for its arrival with a quiet satisfaction? What do I have to lose in this life that I have not already lost? So why this fear of the inevitable?

The door creaked softly. I half-shut my eyes and the blurriness began to dissolve. But no, the door really was opening, very slowly. But it could not be the nurse, she had a quick way about her. So who could it possibly be?

Then I saw Taya.

She looked at me, stopped for a moment, brought her finger to her lips in a quick warning gesture, then noiselessly
shut the door. She wore the same summer dress, white cape
and wide-brimmed straw hat she had worn last summer in
Tiflis. She hesitated near the door for a second then quickly
walked toward me with her feet barely touching the floor. She
came and sat on the edge of my bed, stroked my hair gently
and looked at me with her wonderful intense eyes.

Her face had not changed at all. It gave off the same beauty and radiance as ever. Perhaps the eyes were a shade more
serious, more mature than before, but everything else was
the same.

"Taya…" I whispered hoarsely fighting for air. Suddenly
I was out of breath. "Taya… how have you…"

"Shh…" she said, also in a quick whisper, putting her finger on my mouth. "Don't talk, Shota. Don't say one word. I
know everything, dear. I have been with you all the while,
aching with your pain, crying with your tears and loving you
more and more all the time. Have you forgotten, Shota? We
have one soul between us, and nothing in the world can
cleave it apart, not even death."

I felt an extraordinary sensation of warmth, almost physical warmth, emanating from her every whispered word.
Along with it came the most thrilling sense of complete relax-
ation slowly spreading over my entire body.

"Shota, Shota, my dearest Shota," she continued in the
same quick whisper, looking me straight in my eyes. "I've
been so worried about you… Have you forgotten what
Grandfather told you and Father Shalva and what you yourself have told me so many times? Have you come to doubt
our love? Don't, Shota… It's here just as strong, beautiful
and immortal as ever. This life has been cruel to us, but what
have we lost that is so important? A few little earthly years
that pass like a summer storm, never to linger or return? Was

that all our love was worth; these few dead autumn leaves fluttering in the wind of time?"

She paused momentarily. I wanted to talk, I wanted to say so much to her, but my lips would not move. I found myself completely paralysed by a sudden happiness that descended on me like a benediction. For a second I even thought I was dead, for surely there could not be so much peace in this world... Then she put her delicate hand on my forehead, smoothed it lovingly and I felt the warmth of her flesh. She was alive and so was I. Her words were alive too, each one pulsating with its own passionate conviction.

"I want you to get well, Shota. I want you to get well and strong. I want you to live, to live long and happy, because if you go away, my part of our soul would be cold and lonely without yours. Don't be afraid of life, Shota dear, of all its joys and sorrows; its fluttering good and bad days; its windy nights and black thoughts. It is not difficult at all. No, it is very easy to go through the hardest of lives with a love like ours, which knows no time or death. Live your life through to the end, Shota; to its last sweet or bitter drop. Only then, and only then, my dear, will our one soul come out of life's ordeal strong and free; cleaned of all the tiny impurities of our days on earth. I want you to go back into life without fear, eyes open and head held high, because somewhere in the world I will be loving you, watching you and delighting in your success and courage. Every second I will be proud I have your soul and that you have mine, and that we have each other's hearts. I will be proud that we have never been parted for even one instant... Shota, isn't it wonderful to have something immortal in this mortal world – just as we have? Why then should we decry our fate? We are very lucky, my dear; we are so incredibly lucky, it's the sheerest joy just to think about it."

She laughed softly and happily and suddenly I laughed

too. All my misgivings and despairs evaporated instantly. I felt life flowing back into my body in a great tidal wave. Once again I had everything in the world to live for. I would remain alive and see my life through to its last earthly day.

Meanwhile Taya leaned forward noiselessly and touched my forehead with her soft, warm lips.

"Good-bye, Shota. Live for our love and don't be afraid of anything. Remember that I'm always with you, every second, till we meet again, my dearest dear."

She quickly walked across the room, stopped near the door, gave me a long look, then smiled her usual vibrant smile that made even the sun itself dance. And then she was gone.

I lay there quietly, filled with a strange exaltation. Every fibre of my body tingled with my new and extraordinary happiness. I was afraid to move lest I disturb the enchantment of Taya's presence still lingering in the room.

Then I shut my eyes for a second. When I opened them again bright sunshine flooded into the room. It was morning, but the night nurse was there again, filling in her report sheet at the desk in the corner.

For a moment the change in the room startled me. Then I realised I must have fallen asleep after Taya's visit. Yes Taya's... I remembered it down to its every last detail. Each one of her words and gestures stood out clearly and vividly in my mind. It just couldn't be a dream, but could it truly be reality? Or was it? Cold reason told me no. But from where could I have received this great new sense of well-being? How come a passionate desire to live pervaded my entire body this bright morning? Only one thing was certain; I felt stronger, happier and more confident of recovery now than on any day since my accident.

"Mademoiselle Yvonne," I called quietly.

The nurse turned, put down her pen and approached me. Her long severe face rearranged itself into a kind smile.

"Good morning... How do you feel this morning?"

"Wonderful. I want to ask you something, Mademoiselle. Were you here all night?"

The smile dissolved on her face. "But of course, Monsieur le Prince. Either here or in the little room outside."

"All the time?"

"But of course."

"Did you see anyone come in here during the night?"

An expression of surprise came to her face. "Did anyone come in, Monsieur?"

I smiled. "Then you weren't here all the time? Please tell me."

The nurse hesitated. "I might have stepped out for a few moments Monsieur. You were asleep so peacefully and as I remember it now, I did have a little game of dominoes with Mademoiselle Duval in Room B. But I could hear your bell from there, and I thought..."

The door opened quickly and Doctor Bauer entered, wearing his loose white robe, a medicine bottle in his hand. Erast, looking listless and tired, followed him in and stood near the door. Doctor Bauer walked to the window then started reading the label on the bottle, not even looking at me.

"Good morning, Shota... H'mm... twenty to thirty drops... Your Vasco da Gama has just arrived from Lausanne with this stuff. Took the wrong train back and went pretty nearly all the way round the lake... H'mm, in half a glass of water, every two hours... Give me a glass, Mademoiselle."

He took the glass and started to measure out the dark liquid drop by drop, wrinkling his broad forehead and twisting his nose to keep his glasses from sliding down. He looked touchingly comical, this big, kindly man, ceremoniously manipulating the tiny bottle.

"I've heard before of Doctor Weiss's concoctions. They

are supposed to be very good. This formula for instance..."
He almost dropped the glass when he heard my laughter. He
turned around and his face expressed utter bewilderment.

"I'm sorry, Doctor... You looked so serious there. I just
wanted to inform you that the battle has turned in our favour.
The enemy has been routed and is in full flight. Your ammunition has worked wonders, especially since I've decided to
use it and get well."

As I spoke the expressions on the doctor's face changed
drastically: first to bewilderment; then incredulity; then anxiety; then hope; and finally joy. As I finished my last cheery
sentence he silently emptied the contents of the glass into the
waste pail, then dropped the glass there too for good measure.

"What are you doing?" I asked.

"Throwing this stuff away. I'll be dammed if I let old
Doctor Weiss get another credit for this alchemy.
Mademoiselle! Give me the thermometer!"

My temperature was almost normal. My pulse was
stronger and more regular. My breathing, too, was easier and
steadier than it had been for days.

"Amazing..." Doctor Bauer kept saying. His shaking
hands betrayed the excitement he tried vainly to suppress.
"Absolutely astounding... incredible... I would even say
strange. Just wait a minute, I want Doctor Verne to see this."

He left the room quickly, patting Erast's shoulder as he
went by. Only then I noticed the unusual, tense expression on
Erast's face.

"Erast," I said, "come here."

Erast took a few steps toward me then stopped, erect and
tense. That was not my old Erast. Something had happened.

"What's the matter with you Erast? Have you seen a
ghost?"

"Almost..." he said huskily.

"What nonsense! Come Erast, out with it. What happened?"

Erast squeezed the words out of himself one by one, obviously with great effort. "When I went with that fat doctor last night... I mean, we went past that little hôtel near the depot... I saw him there... He was getting out of a carriage... Bags and all..."

"Who?"

"That man... I mean the gentleman with yellow hair who came to your house in Paris at night..."

"The Baron?"

"Yes, sir."

"Did you speak to him?"

"No sir, I hid behind the fat doctor."

I laughed. I knew that Erast was intensely superstitious and blamed the poor Baron for all the trouble which had come our way since his visit. "Erast, Erast, you're incorrigible... So the Baron is in Vevey. It's a strange coincidence, but there is nothing to be afraid of. In fact, I'd like to see him! Mademoiselle," I turned to the nurse and switched into French. "May I have your pen and a piece of paper?"

I quickly wrote a short note informing the Baron that I was in Doctor Verne's clinic and inviting him to visit me at his convenience. I waited until the ink was dry then folded the paper, put it into an envelope and turned to Erast.

"You will take this to..."

I did not finish because I saw Erast's face. Every muscle in it was frozen and large clear tears were rolling down his weather-bitten cheeks then losing themselves in the dense, scraggly jungle of his moustache.

"Erast... what's the matter?"

Erast did not answer, but our eyes met for an instant. Then I looked down at the envelope which I was turning between my fingers. There was a short pause while I gathered my inner strength.

"Erast…" I said in a very low voice, broken with emotion. "Erast… The Baron… was not alone?"

I looked up at Erast. The expression on his face had not changed, but the tears were now coming at much quicker intervals and looked bigger…

I tore the note into very small bits and dropped them into the waste basket beside my bed.

Ten

TERESA

True love in this differs as gold from clay,
That to divide is not to take away.

SHELLEY

MY recovery progressed apace, but the long siege of the pneumonia had left my system weakened and exhausted. Doctor Bauer strongly advised me to spend several months at least in Davos before returning to active life. The doctor felt that the healthy air of the famous mountain retreat, which had once saved my life as a child, would be highly beneficial again. I sensed he could be right. Besides, I had become attached to him during my illness – so happily accepted the invitation to become his guest in Davos for as long as necessary.

Doctor Bauer departed from Vevey as soon as my condition left no doubt at all of my position on the road to recovery. Anxious to return to his clinic, he felt sure that Doctor Verne could handle my case until I proved strong enough for the trip across Switzerland.

Autumn had already painted the mountainsides with every

hue of magenta and gold when they finally discharged me from the clinic. Accompanied by my faithful Erast, I then left for Davos.

But I had emerged from Vevey a very different man. For one, I had matured, both physically and mentally. The emotional euphoria that followed Taya's nocturnal visit, whether real or unreal, dissipated gradually. But the sense of peace and sober determination to live remained. No longer was I disturbed by spells of bitterness and despair, but at the same time all the natural desires of my youth seemed to have abandoned my body. This left my soul with an old man's feeling of satisfaction and calm. My temper evened out, was no longer broken by emotional outbursts or periods of brooding depression. I presented a cheerful and unusually considerate persona to everyone I met. But somehow the deeper joy of living had departed from my soul. I accepted the arrival of each new day as just another milestone to be passed with the least mental disturbance, then laid safely away in the storehouse of memory.

I found it pleasant to return to the beautiful Davos valley where every stone, tree and hill brought back recollections of my youth. I had many friends there. But after our first meetings – usually noisy and embarrassing – we rarely met again. During my short year of absence all inner connection between us seemed to have been broken. My comrades, some older than I, now seemed very young, almost infantile in their appetites for life – which I somehow no longer shared. Gradually they all drifted away to leave me alone with Doctor Bauer, Erast and the countless books in Doctor Bauer's excellent library.

My life became monotonous and well ordered. In the mornings I would ride or walk with Erast; and later, when snow had blanketed the mountains, ski or skate. My afternoons were spent either in the doctor's library or at the desk in my room. The backlog of business reports from Samourzakani and France had mounted up during my illness and many things required attention. There were serious problems and trifling ones, but one letter in particular caught my attention. Addressed to Grandfather and marked 'personal,' it contained a bill from a Budapest florist for 'your annual order for black roses to be delivered daily to your chapel at St. Stephen cemetery.' I immediately forwarded the money and asked the florist to render all future bills to me.

But it was evening time that I cherished most. Doctor Bauer would return from the clinic and after dinner we would adjourn to the drawing-room, sit before a roaring fire, drink coffee, play draughts or just talk. Draughts was Doctor Bauer's passion. He played the game with great concentration and seriousness, but indifferent skill. He took every defeat with such a genuine display of unhappiness that I was careful to win as infrequently as possible. The longer I knew the doctor the more I loved and respected him. There in the sanctity of his home he showed a quite different side from the silent and efficient doctor I had known as a young man. I soon began to see the subtle and generous heart that lay behind his erudition and professionalism. Also how down through the years he had retained a childlike capacity for enthusiasm and a powerful ability to empathise with the feelings of other people. His concern for his patients often showed itself as highly personal. Many times I saw him rejoicing at their successes or else becoming inconsolable at some bad news from the bedside.

One evening he returned home late and I immediately saw that something troubled him. We dined in silence, then when left alone in the drawing room he suddenly turned to me, only to then hesitate as he battled to find the right words.

"Shota," he said finally, "I am going to ask you a personal question, but please if you think it impertinent, don't answer. But I mean… how are your prayers, my boy?"

"Prayers?" I asked, somewhat taken aback.

"Yes... you pray, don't you?"

"Every night."

"Well what I mean is... do you feel that your prayers are listened to by... er... God, or are they just mechanical acts of devotion as with so many other people?"

Clearly he felt very awkward. This famous scientist who had worked all his life with the physical conditions of the human body, now addressed something far removed from the conventional concepts of science.

"I don't know," I said honestly. "There are days when I feel close to God and days I feel less. But I do believe that every genuinely earnest prayer will be heard... and answered, if it is offered up sincerely."

"Shota," he said, in a low voice now charged with real anguish, "I have a boy at the clinic. He's dying just as surely as you were dying that night in Vevey. Medicine can't help him any longer. I have prayed but I'm not such a religious man... He needs better prayers than mine... Could you, Shota...?"

I was deeply touched. "I will pray," I promised. "What is his name Doctor?"

"Ho Rhan... His father is a Cambodian philosopher. He's a truly good person."

"But Doctor... is he a Christian?"

Doctor Bauer stared at me through his glasses. "No Shota, but he's made by God just like you and me."

His words made me feel bitterly ashamed.

Little by little I came to understand what had made Doctor Bauer such an excellent physician. It lay in his instinctive belief in a spiritual element to human life and the power of its influence over the human body.

"I am a doctor," he told me once, "and my business is the mending of human bodies. Outside of that I'm an ignoramus. But I would be a poor physician indeed if I thought that man was nothing more than cells and molecules. Just as a carriage maker would be a fool if he thought that the moment his carriage falls to pieces all its components disappear into thin air."

My days went by peacefully inside Doctor Bauer's big brown house. I became so accustomed to its measured routine that I looked with apprehension toward the time I would have to leave Davos and return to my own life.

After an unsettled period of cloudy autumn skies and snowstorms, the weather crystallized to produce the perfectly clear days that made the Davos valley such a Mecca for winter sports. The mountains, now covered with a thick blanket of powdery snow, stood out like giant slabs of white sugar against an intensely blue sky. Around them the air sparkled like white wine. Throngs of tourists began to swarm into hôtel lobbies and mountain lodges as the winter season relaunched itself – to the swish of skis by day and the clink of punch glasses at night.

Skating had always been one of my favourite sports and as soon as the weather permitted I spent two or three hours every morning on the frozen pond. Erast was at first reluctant to venture onto the ice, but after two or three bad falls he quickly discovered his skating legs. From that moment on he lost all sense of restraint. He treated his skates like two stunt horses, and the skating rink, a 'jiritoba' arena. Other skaters scattered before him as he raced through the crowd like a mountain dervish. His sense of timing proved alarmingly good and gave him the ability to avoid terrible collisions right at the last second, before whirring away into the crowd like a speeding bullet.

I, alas, could not boast such prowess despite all my experience. Then one morning, when a young woman skater bore down on me, I found myself totally unable to avoid crashing into her. The impact sent her whirling out of control through the crowd. When she finally slid to a halt she stayed sitting on the ice nursing one of her legs. I sped over and discovered a beautiful young woman of perhaps twenty wearing a smart woollen skating suit; with spun-gold hair spilling out from under her knitted cap.

"Oh he killed me…" she said in English, rubbing her leg, quite unaware of my presence.

At that moment Erast arrived and we started to help her back to her feet – a familiarity fully accepted on every skating rink the world over.

"I am terribly sorry," I told her also in English. "So clumsy of me…"

"It was my fault really… oh!" she groaned as she tried to stand on the injured leg. "I'm afraid you'll have to help me to the side."

We did so. She sat on the bench and tried to flex her leg, which fortunately worked.

"Can you help me take off the skates?" she asked me with a helplessness which I found charming, "I'm afraid I'm through for today."

I knelt down and began to unscrew her skates.

"Are you an Englishman?" she asked.

I looked at her more closely. Her features were delicate and her eyes incredibly blue and direct.

"No," I said.

"Still you have an English accent."

"I'm from the Caucasus."

"I'm an American," she said. "My name is Teresa Magawely but my father calls me Tress."

I introduced myself and she gave me her hand. Her handshake was firm, almost manly.

"I'm very glad that you speak English so well," she said. "My German is nil, my French rusty. I think my foot is all right now. This is my first day on skates."

"Have you been here long?"

"Since last night. My father has some business here. Among other things he manufactures winter sports equipment in Baltimore. Now he's touring the European sporting venues acquainting himself with prospective new victims."

She laughed. It was the closest to Taya's laughter I had heard since we'd parted. It carried the same sense of complete abandon and my heart gave a spasmodic leap in my chest. All of a sudden the day around me seemed brighter and the sky bluer; almost the same blue as that in Teresa's eyes.

She stood up, walked slowly around, limping slightly.

"I'm definitely all right," she declared cheerily. "Thank you very much for your help."

"Here are your skates Miss Magawely," I said, handing them back.

"Thank you."

Then suddenly she looked around and spotting a bedraggled boy of about fifteen sitting on the bench staring at the skaters, she called to him; "Kommen sie hier." The boy approached gingerly then she handed him the skates. "A gift from America," she said. The boy almost fell over with astonishment. He thanked her almost disbelievingly then walked away, at first slowly, then faster and faster. She watched him and laughed again.

"Dear boy… Do you want to walk me home?" Her manner was sincere and direct, but without any undue forwardness. Everything she said and did seemed to possess a simple and intrinsic dignity.

"I'd be very happy."

I removed my skates quickly and handed them to Erast – who wanted to accompany us, but I told him to go home and wait for me there.

"What language did you speak, Russian?" Teresa asked.

"No, Georgian. We are from Georgia."

"Uh-oh!" she laughed. "Don't let Father hear about it. He went right through Atlanta with Sherman. The very word makes him see red."

"I won't," I promised.

Teresa and I started up the slope leading to the street, talking and laughing. She had an amazing faculty of immediately putting people at their ease. In a few moments I felt I had known her all my life. I wanted to hire a sleigh but Teresa preferred to walk. She no longer limped and promised all the pain had gone, that she never felt better in her life. As for myself, I realised I felt young again. Suddenly I wanted to live and to laugh.

The Magawelys stayed at the Palace Hôtel of Davos, a sprawling chalet-like affair located on the outskirts of the main village, and set directly against a majestic backdrop of white hills. Not a long walk, but by the time we reached the hôtel I already knew a great deal about Teresa and her family. Her mother was dead and her father an impoverished Irish nobleman who had created a new home across the Atlantic. He had made his fortune in the New World only to watch it wiped out during the 1893 American Panic. Now he fought an uphill battle to regain his former status.

We stood talking in front of the hôtel until finally Teresa, obviously growing cold, suggested I come in for a moment to meet her father. I accepted.

Colonel James Patrick Magawely was a giant of a man and his huge frame housed so much charm and ebullience, I liked him from the first moment he clasped my hand. He possessed the same blue eyes as Teresa, the geniality and wit of my grandfather, and the eloquence of the Blarney Stone. In some imperceptible way he combined the solid culture of the old world with the effervescent enthusiasm and vigour of the new – his adopted home – which he described with great warmth and attachment. But what impressed me most was the deep and instinctive understanding between him and his daughter – a camaraderie that seemed based on a mutual respect and complete devotion.

Colonel Magawely insisted on my staying for lunch and the three of us took an informal meal in front of an open fireplace. The Colonel did most of the talking. First he questioned me about Russia and I quickly discovered him better informed than I on the economic problems of the country. Then he switched to American politics, delivering a vociferous condemnation of President Cleveland and his Democratic administration, which according to him had wrecked the economic life of the nation. He predicted a complete Republican sweep in the next election.

I knew precious little about American politics but enjoyed Colonel Magawely's harangue, largely because it gave me the chance to engage in a charmingly silent game with Teresa. She would throw the laughing blue sparks of her eyes in my direction and I would try to catch them across the table, while retaining my attitude as attentive listener. This sport continued throughout the lunch and I am afraid much of Colonel Magawely's excellent oratory was wasted on me.

Finally I returned home having made an appointment to fetch Teresa the next morning for a sleigh ride down the Landwasserstrasse. I arrived back in my rooms a quite different man from the one who walked out of Doctor Bauer's house that morning. All the Hamlet-like melancholy had evaporated, to be replaced by renewed appetites.

Erast met me in my room and helped me change clothes. I felt a strong need to talk to someone but all attempts at conversation failed. He seemed sullen and morose. Finally I demanded an explanation. After some hard pressing Erast cast his eyes downward and muttered:

"I had a dream last night and it made me sad."

"What dream?"

I had to repeat the question at least half a dozen times before Erast mumbled his answer:

"I saw Princess Taya on a white horse. She was so beautiful that I cried all night."

That was all I could get out of Erast. But I understood him perfectly. Deep down in his soul he censured me for disloyalty to Taya. For a moment the thought disturbed me too. But then I dismissed it. Nothing serious or sinful existed in my friendship with Teresa. Besides didn't Taya want me to be happy? Surely just another amusing quirk of Erast's psychology, I told myself, nothing more. How could I ever forget Taya?

But as the days passed I began to find all my thoughts wrapping themselves around Tress. It was by no means the intense electric attraction I had felt for Taya – but a beautiful thing none the less; a friendship in the best and noblest sense of the word. I experienced it as an attachment between two young human beings who found complete companionship in each other's company. Behind the outward show of minor eccentricity, I found in Tress an excellent and stimulating mind capable of profound thought.

Gradually the idea of parting with Tress began to worry me. Whenever it occurred I immediately banished it from my mind, unable to process the fact in any rational way. My only technique was simply to continue enjoying each beautiful day as it rolled past.

Then came the evening when I discovered Tress felt exactly the same. I met her in the lobby of her hôtel but this time she greeted me with a new and crestfallen look.

"Father had a cable from Washington," she said in a hollow voice. "We are going home."

The words hit me so abruptly and unexpectedly that at first I didn't catch their meaning.

"When?" I asked mechanically.

"In the morning."

Then my heart suddenly sank and I understood with absolute clarity that I loved her.

"But it can't be…" I muttered. "Don't you understand… my God, Tress… it just can't happen!"

"I know," she said soberly. "Let's go somewhere where we can talk."

Silently we climbed into a sleigh and drove to a mountain lodge some two or three kilometres out of Platz, the main village of Davos. We ordered hot wine with sugar, cinnamon and cloves then retreated to a secluded room, separated from the main floor by a sliding door. Here we knew we would not be disturbed by the après-ski merry-makers or wandering Tyrolean troubadours in the main room.

We sat down and looked squarely at each other. "You can't go," I told her flatly.

"Father needs me. Can't you come with us?"

"I don't know. Doctor Bauer says I should stay here until the spring. Can't you talk to your father and stay here?"

She thought for second. "I'll stay if you say I should. But Father is going through a crucial moment of his career and needs me. He depends on me. It wouldn't be right to leave him now."

"Very well. But Tress, I'll be so lonely without you."

"Just for a little while?"

"How little?"

"Until Father's business is more secure. Then I'll come here, or you come there, it doesn't matter."

I took her hand and kissed it.

"I'm going with you tomorrow, Tress."

"But you can't. Your health…"

"An ocean voyage would do me good. Then we'll come back here together, stay for a while before going to the Caucasus. I love you, Tress."

"I love you, Shota."

"I must order the tickets for Erast and me."

We looked at each other and suddenly laughed.

Our communion was interrupted by a loud commotion in the main room. The music stopped abruptly, to be replaced by a chorus of respectful greetings. We turned and through the open door saw a tall and handsome young man wearing a black cape with sable collars step into the lodge accompanied by three men carrying guitars and a violin. The young man was obviously well known because he instantly became the focus of everyone's attention, and was then ceremoniously conducted to a small table beside the fireplace. The musicians sat in a semicircle behind him, extracted their instruments from their cases and began tuning them.

"Who is that?" Tress asked.

"That is a very sad story," I said. "Let's leave."

"Tell me Shota. I want to know."

So I told her the story as I had heard it from Doctor Bauer and others. The young man was a compatriot of mine, one Count Troganoff, the only heir to one of the great fortunes of Europe. A brilliant officer of the Cavalry Guards, he found himself stricken by tuberculosis a few years ago and was now dying in Davos. He decided to drown his last days in wine and gypsy music provided by the private orchestra he brought with him from the Russian capital. Doctor Bauer told me his condition was hopeless. The young man knew it too but determinedly filled his last hours on earth with gaiety and gusto.

Tears came to Tress's sky-blue eyes as she listened to the story. She put her hand on mine and held it firmly.

"Shota, it's so good to be young, alive and in love."

Then the champagne bottles started to pop, as was the usual procedure. Wherever the dying Count appeared wine began to flow and everyone in the establishment was invited to join the bacchanal.

"Shall we go?" I asked Tress again.

"Let's stay just for a few more moments," she said.

One of the musicians, a dark-haired violinist, stepped forward, swung up his instrument and gypsy music started to fill the room. Suddenly my heart contracted painfully. He played the very song that Taya performed on my apartment's piano; the same song the young Ishtvan Irmey played repeatedly to that young Georgian nobleman in Budapest many years earlier. It brought the presence of Taya back to me so vividly I felt we had never parted. I realised with a paralysing shock that Taya had not left my life in any way, nor ever could.

"What a beautiful piece," Tress whispered.

I said nothing, just pulled my hand out of hers and stood up. She realised then that something had happened. I put some money on the table and walked quickly towards a side door with Teresa following.

The night outside was clear, cold and top-heavy with stars. I helped Tress into the waiting sleigh, pulled the fur cover up to our chins and told the driver to ride down the valley and just keep going. The icy air cut into our faces and Teresa moved close to me, instinctively seeking warmth and comfort. Violently conflicting emotions tore at my heart. I loved Teresa, she was the dearest human being in the whole world to me – outside of Taya. But I felt deeply, terribly sorry for her. Why had fate been so unjust as to send into her path this empty shell of a man whose very soul no longer belonged to him?

"Tress my darling," I spoke softly into her ear, now so close to my lips, "there is something I must tell you, because I love you too much to cause you even a second of unhappiness. Tress… please try to understand."

At first haltingly and incoherently, then in a more orderly

way, I told her the whole story about Taya and in every detail – starting with our meeting in Tiflis, up to the spectral night when she entered my hospital room in Vevey. Teresa listened intently without interruption, not missing a single word. We drove many kilometres down into the valley, then I told the driver to turn back. My story ended just as we approached the main village of Davos.

"Now you know everything, Tress, as much as I know. But I hope you understand it better than I. Surely you now know why you must go away and forget me. Your life is too young, splendid and precious to be wasted on someone who carries someone else's soul in him. One who can never give you what you so richly deserve – his whole undivided devotion and love. For Tress, and this is God's truth, I will never stop loving Taya for as long as I live and not even after that."

A silence descended on us, filled only with the sound of the horse's hooves on the packed snow and the creaking of the runners. Far ahead the lights of Platz glittered in the frosty air.

I felt Teresa turn towards me. She took my head between her gloved hands and in the dim starlight I saw her face close to mine. Then she spoke to me slowly and deliberately.

"I loved you very much when we drove out of the hôtel tonight, but I love you infinitely more now. Then I loved you for yourself, now I love you also for your love for Taya. I don't want you ever to forget her, Shota, because if you did you wouldn't be the man I love. Neither do I want to take her place in your heart. But I believe and know that my love could live in your heart side by side with Taya's. I also know that Taya would be happier knowing that you were not alone in this world. I know that because I understand Taya as no one else does. Because, Shota, I love you the same way Taya does."

Her words touched the very depths of my soul. I sat

motionless for a second, then I put my arms around her and touched her cold lips with mine.

"Tress," I said, trying desperately to put my thoughts in order. "I cannot solve this problem by myself. If I didn't love you the way that I do, everything would be simple. But I love you, and now everything is difficult. Go home and wait for me. If I ever come, I will bring you my untroubled heart or I won't come at all. You understand don't you?"

"I do," she said simply. "And I'll wait for you."

Our sleigh arrived at the entrance to the hôtel. I escorted Teresa to the door and as I kissed her hand she smiled. I could feel a great and patient understanding in that smile.

"Don't hurry, Shota. Search and find your peace, then come back to me when you are ready. I'll be waiting for you with my love."

She bit her lip, turned and almost ran inside. The oaken door swung shut heavily behind her.

It was past midnight when I arrived home. Doctor Bauer had already gone to bed, but Erast as always was waiting for me. I went to my room and sat on the edge of my bed.

"Erast," I said wearily, running my hand across my forehead, "get our things ready. We are leaving in the morning."

"Yes, sir,' said Erast dispassionately, kneeling and pulling off my shoes.

Eleven

FATHER VARLAAM

IN all my years of life I had never seen my native Samourzakani in its winter clothes. As a child we always spent our winters in Tiflis or Switzerland. Taya and I had come there in late summer. In my mind Samourzakani was always associated with hot days and the heady smell of flowers and fresh hay.

But beauty is beauty wherever it is and in whatever attire. As our train closed in on our destination, I found myself completely enchanted again by my country. In spite of the fact that the orderly rows of vines looked bare and scraggly along the castle slopes, and the sky spread out flat and grey, the countryside had not lost its beauty. Great pines and cedars, laden with fresh snow stood like sentinels on the mountain-sides. Underneath them the earth itself seemed to emit a vine-like odour, hinting at the new and vigorous growth gathering strength beneath the cold winter blanket.

Vano Maradze met us at the station. He looked slightly older and a shadow of worry now lay across his face. His usually pointed black moustache was no longer waxed, and drooped mournfully.

I embraced him warmly. Maradze was a faithful friend and also the living spokesman of my native land, just like Erast and the sober-faced peasants sitting beside their bundles on the platform.

"I have your horses outside," he told me in an immensely improved French, obviously used for the benefit of the peasants on the platform. "And I kept your arrival a secret, just as you asked in your telegram. Even Agathe doesn't know."

"How is she?" I asked with a smile.

Deep anxiety appeared on Maradze's face. "She is expecting our child any time now... I hope to God everything will be all right."

Immediately I understood his uncharacteristic nervousness and unkempt appearance. "It will be," I tried to assure him. "These things have been done before. You are a lucky man. You will have a wonderful child. You already have a fine wife."

"I know it," Maradze nodded.

Our baggage was loaded onto the creaking cart and we started off for the castle. The further we drove the more beautiful the countryside became. When we finally approached the swirling Ingur river we stopped to admire the black ribbon of angry water as it twisted its way down from the snowy hills.

Samourzakani waited for us on the other side like a lovely bride wearing a virginal veil of white snow.

I looked at Erast. His face expressed no emotion, but his eyes were wide and intense, full of the rolling hills and pastures which now stretched away in the wintry haze beyond the river. When the ferry finally touched the far bank he dismounted slowly, knelt down and reverently kissed the snow of his motherland. There was such simple dignity in that gesture I felt tears welling up in my eyes.

We arrived at the castle toward evening. Maradze found

his wife well and in good spirits – which cheered him no end. He even suggested we start the process of checking his accounts, but I begged him to relent for a few days, because although I felt very tired I had another mission. My first task would be to reach some kind of resolution for the chaos of my own emotions. Until this had been achieved I could make no serious decisions.

I walked through the empty halls and spacious rooms of the castle, thinking. Everything reminded me of Taya and Grandfather – the simple, happy part of my life which was now gone forever. Then I thought of Teresa somewhere on the high seas on her way to America – and my heart ached. I knew that she longed for me as much as I longed for her. But try as I might I could see no way out of the labyrinth which wrapped itself so tightly around my soul.

I slept fitfully that night, most of the time waiting for morning. When finally it dawned it brought with it a strong northern wind which picked up the particles of icy dust and hurled them through the air at everything. Maradze predicted a blizzard before nightfall, but fortunately his forecasting proved no better than anyone else's. By mid-afternoon the wind died away and a perfectly blue sky sparkled out over Samourzakani. I called Erast, who had already changed into his traditional dress, and told him to saddle our horses. Half an hour later we rode out over the castle bridge and headed up into the hills.

The roads were icy and covered with a thin coating of snow which made riding slow and difficult. We successfully negotiated the narrow trail where two summers ago our party found itself trapped behind the rock slide. Then I reined in my horse.

"Erast," I said, "turn back and go to the castle. Tell Mr. Maradze not to worry. I am going to spend the night at Iliori. Meet me in the morning right here under this pine."

"I shall go with you, Master."

"No, Erast, I must be alone."

"The trails are hard to find, Master. I shall go with you."

I put my hand on his shoulder. "Listen to me, Erast. You are the only man who knows the sorrow of my life. Now I need to talk to the only man who can show me the way through. For this I must be alone. Go back and don't worry. I can find the way. In the morning I'll be here under this tree."

I turned my horse and rode away along the narrow trail up the hill. When I reached the top I stopped and looked back. The figure of Erast and his horse stood where I left them silhouetted against the snow as small as a toy. I waved to Erast and he waved back – but it seemed different to his usual gesture. From where I stood it looked like the sign of the cross. I continued on toward the monastery which from my memory I knew existed somewhere beyond the next chain of hills.

But I had over-estimated my sense of direction. Soon I found myself hopelessly lost. I rode and rode but the old monastery just never appeared. I turned back, rode left then right, crossed and recrossed the trails, but all I ever saw were yet more white hills dotted with green and black trees. They all looked maddeningly similar. Then the sun began to set and pools of blackness started gathering down in the valleys. Before I knew it night suddenly arrived and when I looked up I saw the sky now sprinkled with thousands of stars.

I stopped my tired horse and tried to work out any possible solution to what was now a serious predicament. The problem was, even if I wanted to turn back I'd no chance of even finding my own castle. I thought I knew the general direction and peered out into the darkness trying to spot anything vaguely familiar from the rows of mountain outlines. Then suddenly I noticed a tiny flickering light in the near distance. With my eyes fixed on it, I rode swiftly across a gentle ravine and soon recognised the half-ruined wall of the old monastery looming straight ahead. It seemed I had lost my way less than a kilometre from my destination.

I dismounted and led my horse up in the direction of the gate. True enough I soon came up to the lantern burning behind the gate's iron grille. I heard the rattle of heavy bolts and a voice I recognized at once.

"Tie your horse to the gate, my son. One of the brothers will take care of it."

I followed these instructions and entered the monastery yard. Father Shalva stood there tall and erect, staff in one hand, lantern in the other. The flickering light of his candle cast an unsteady glow on his ancient face and thin white beard.

"What brings you here at this hour of the night?"

"I come to seek your advice, Father."

I bowed my head and Father Shalva placed the lantern on the ground and blessed me. Then he picked it up again.

"Follow me."

We walked across the yard, entered a dark building and headed down a vaulted corridor.

"This way..."

He opened a door and led me into a small room – most probably his own cell. No more than a cold stone cubicle of about three metres square, it stood almost completely bare, save for a small altar and a row of icons. A narrow straw bed also lay in the corner neatly covered with a grey blanket and nearby a small oak bench leaned against one of the walls. The cell had no windows and water dripped from its rough granite walls.

Father Shalva shut the door and blew out the lantern. The only light that remained came from the shivering tongues of the icon lamps reflecting brightly from the gold of the images. The silence was complete and time seemed suddenly to have been shut outside beyond the door.

Father Shalva appeared virtually unchanged since my last visit. The years had made little impression on his age-less face. Only his eyes perhaps looked slightly more sunken under the bony eaves of his brow, and his beard whiter and thinner. But his body retained its strangely youthful agility. He leant his staff in the corner, removed his black calotte and hung it on the wall, then loosened the tight collar of his cassock. Sitting on one end of the bench he smiled kindly.

"Sit down and let me hear your story. God will find the way to bring peace into your heart if you open it fully to Him."

I sat down on the other end of the bench. Father Shalva cast his eyes down onto the ground and prepared to listen. His parchment-like face took on the expression of great serenity and his body beneath seemed to adopt the stillness of a marble statue. Indeed the only factor to break this illusion was his ancient withered hand that occasionally moved to stroke his beard.

"I am listening."

I had prepared my story beforehand, but sitting there I found it impossible to follow any of its prearranged narrative. Instead my emotions crowded the words out through my mouth in a turbulent hot stream. I spoke of Taya and my eternal love for her, of my love for Teresa, and how these two deep and sincere loves had become so hopelessly entwined. I explained how my soul could no longer distinguish where one ended and the other began. It was an incoherent tale of mental and emotional anguish, and it poured out of my heart without any logic or continuity.

Finally, when all was told I stopped and looked up. Father Shalva remained sitting silently before me as before, without moving. The silence grew and grew. I could hear the blood rushing through my temples, sounding like the dull roar of an incoming tide. But still Father Shalva remained sitting silently.

Eventually he raised his eyes and looked straight at me. I felt the simple clean strength of that gaze as his words came at me distinct and clear.

"I have listened to your words. You have spoken of two loves that live side by side in your heart. You have spoken of Taya's love, Teresa's, and your own, as if there were many different loves in this world. But my son, true love is but one; not Taya's, not Teresa's, not yours or mine, but God's. If it is true love that you have in your soul it will never be divided; never wither or perish. Who knows, perhaps God in His wisdom has chosen you to receive a double measure of His munificence. Then you must accept this great responsibility with gratitude and humility, without misgiving or fears."

He paused, gazed at the small altar, then continued.

"True love, which permeates and moves all God's creation on this earth and above, is also His handiwork. As such it possesses a measurelessness and a unity which cannot be broken or held in private ownership. The moment it is torn to pieces it loses its godliness and immortality, becomes impure and subject to decay and destruction.

"There is one God. He is endless, timeless, measureless, and all His handiwork is endless and measureless and cannot be divided. Yet man in his blinded greed for things he can call his own, refuses to embrace this oneness. Instead he attempts to break it into many pieces, take these segments away and proclaim each for his own. He fails to understand that what he treasures so much as living segments of God's creation, become merely soulless, dead things, devoid of all purpose and worth the moment they are detached from God."

He stopped for a minute, then his severe countenance melted and he added in a softer voice:

"Don't be disturbed by doubts, my son. For if Taya's love

is true, it is also Teresa's. If Teresa's is true, it is also Taya's, because both are one, and both are God's."

For a moment I was speechless, then I gathered my thoughts.

"Then Father..." I began haltingly, but Father Shalva interrupted me gently.

"Yes, my son. It matters not at all to God which one of the two women you love and take for your earthly bride. But it matters everything to Him if you ever allow unfaithfulness to poison the true love which He has entrusted to your keeping."

Suddenly I felt as if a great weight had just fallen from my soul. In its place an enormous wave of joy seemed to all but sweep me from my feet.

"Thank you, Father," I whispered.

The old man rose. I bowed my head again and again he blessed me. I took his wrinkled hand and kissed it with reverence and gratitude.

"Now I shall show you to your bed," he said, taking hold of his staff.

I walked with him to the door, then suddenly a thought struck me. I stopped dead and the old man looked back at me expectantly.

"Father..." I said, hesitating and trying to choose the right words. "The woman I love is of a different faith."

Father Shalva knitted his white eyebrows.

"What different faith?"

"She's a Catholic, Father."

The Father's brows remained stormily knit. "I'm surprised at you, my son, and grieved. What faith is there but the Faith? Did not our Lord Jesus Christ bring ten Gospels into the world? Men, and only men, have cleaved it ten different ways, each for his own."

Father Shalva then put his arm around me and led me out of the cell. We walked along a dark corridor and he opened the door of another very small cell, dimly illuminated with an icon lamp. The small room was completely bare save for a heap of straw in the corner.

"Lay down and sleep. Straw is not the softest bed in the world but Our Lord found it comfortable enough on His first day on earth."

Father Shalva blessed me again and walked out of the cell, closing the door behind him. I was so emotionally exhausted and so physically tired, I collapsed straight down onto the straw, where a merciful sleep enveloped me at once.

When I opened my eyes the glorious light of a new day poured in through the slit of the cell's narrow window. In this radiance the room looked even poorer than on the previous night. The bare walls were covered with mould and dripped water, yet I felt serenely happy.

I sat up trying to take in everything that had happened. Erast would now be waiting for me under the big pine. We would ride to the castle and I would send a man to the station with a telegram destined for Baltimore telling Tress I was on the way to join her. I rose to my feet, humming a happy tune and shook the loose straws from my clothes.

I walked out into the corridor, now dark and deserted and found myself having virtually to grope my way to the door of Father Shalva's cell. I knocked but received no response, so pushing it ajar I found the room empty save for the shimmering light of the icon lamps. I stepped inside and gazed at the altar. Among the relics of Greek Orthodox saints I noticed a small statue of Saint Teresa of Avila.

I knelt before the altar and said a short prayer. Then I walked out into the corridor again and noticed daylight pouring in through cracks in the door at the far end. This time I found my way without difficulty. When I opened the door I was immediately blinded by the whiteness of the snow and blueness of the sky.

It took my eyes several seconds to acclimatise to the riot of light. Then I noticed that I stood in the monastery yard. My horse, looking rested and fit, was standing by the wall as a young man in a black cassock saddled it with the swift movements of a skilled mountain rider.

"Good morning, Father..." I began. The man looked at me and smiled from behind his neatly trimmed beard.

"...Father Varlaam," he helped me complete my sentence. "I hope you spent a restful night?"

"Quite, Father, thank you. What is the shortest way from here to the Samourzakani road?"

The monk thought for a few seconds. "The trails are covered with snow. But if you follow this brook to the grove of cedars down the valley then turn left and cut across the ravine you can't go wrong. Go straight ahead until you come upon a road, then turn right and follow it all the way to the castle."

I thanked him and he handed me the reins of my horse.

"One moment," I said, handing back the reins. "I must take my leave of Father Shalva first. Where do you suppose I might find him?"

Father Varlaam looked at me bewildered. "Father Shalva?"

"Yes."

The monk blinked several times. "But Father Shalva died," he said simply.

"When?" I whispered unsteadily.

The monk looked at the fleecy clouds floating across the sky.

"Last Easter, almost a year ago."

I swung myself into the saddle and rode out of the monastery, following the bubbling brook.

Twelve

THE BARONESS AGAIN

THE old Baroness turned the page and discovered it the last.

Carefully she stacked the yellowish sheets together then bound them again in the soft wrapping paper with its worn creases. She placed the neat package down on the table beside her then looked around for the first time in two or three hours.

The snow-capped mountains of Samourzakani melted away before her eyes, giving way to the upstairs room of the Café de la Colombe in Paris. Her coffee had remained untouched, now cold and covered with a whitish film of milk. But to her it looked strangely like the fresh ice spread across the frozen pond at Davos. Then gradually she absorbed the changes in the world around her.

For one thing the day outside had grown older. The infantile blueness of the sky had transformed into a tarnished version of its former self. The smoke from a million chimneys had diluted its colour to a greyish-blue, and a lonely aeroplane now struggled across its emptiness toward the horizon.

The waiter with reddish hair and freckled pug-nose noticed the Baroness and glided over to her table.

"Do you want anything more, Madame?"

The Baroness looked up at him and suddenly felt as if an ancient page of her youth had just reopened. The waiter's face was so hauntingly familiar.

"François…" the Baroness whispered as though talking to herself. "No, this couldn't be François…"

"Oh no Madame," said the waiter. "I am Gaston. François is my father. He used to work here many years ago."

"Where is he now?"

"At home, Madame. He retired right after the Stavitsky affair. His eyes became bad. Anything you wish, Madame?"

The Baroness opened her bag, fumbled through it for a few seconds then lifted out an old nickel-plated waiter's badge. It had lost its original lustre long ago. The nickel had worn off in several spots but the number '9' was still easily visible.

"Please give this to your father, Gaston," said the Baroness, handing the badge to the waiter.

He took it doubtfully.

"Yes, Madame."

The Baroness extracted a banknote and placed it beside her cold coffee.

"Ask him if he remembers two young lovers who came here once, when he too was young. He gave this badge to them as a token of good luck. He will remember."

The Baroness rose, lifted the wrapped manuscript from the table, looked at the confused waiter and suddenly smiled.

"Be sure and tell him that his token worked well; that they had a long and very happy life."

"Yes, Madame."

She turned and walked across the room toward the door, wonderfully tall and erect, slowly and imperiously, like an old queen who had held her last court.